He'd saved her life.

He'd done so efficiently, with practiced ease, a true professional. And it just occurred to her that she hadn't even thanked him. She'd been too focused on figuring out why he was there and how much he would interfere with her private investigation.

"Thank you," she yelled through the door. "For everything."

He seemed sharply efficient while staying studiously detached. But then there were those acts of unexpected kindness, the shirt in her left hand, the small bag of essentials in the other, room service.

Brant Law wasn't an easy man to figure out.

But she'd be damned if he thought she'd give up trying....

DANA MARTON

IRONCLAD COVER

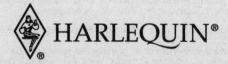

HARLEQUIN®

TORONTO • NEW YORK • LONDON
AMSTERDAM • PARIS • SYDNEY • HAMBURG
STOCKHOLM • ATHENS • TOKYO • MILAN • MADRID
PRAGUE • WARSAW • BUDAPEST • AUCKLAND

With many thanks to Denise Zaza,
Allison Lyons and Maggie Scillia.

ISBN-13: 978-0-373-69258-3
ISBN-10:   0-373-69258-7

IRONCLAD COVER

Copyright: © 2007 by Dana Marton

ABOUT THE AUTHOR

Author Dana Marton lives near Wilmington, Delaware. She has been an avid reader since childhood and has a master's degree in writing popular fiction. When not writing, she can be found either in her garden or her home library. For more information on the author and her other novels, please visit her Web site at www.danamarton.com.

She would love to hear from her readers via e-mail: DanaMarton@yahoo.com.

Books by Dana Marton

CAST OF CHARACTERS

Anita Caballo—Her life was torn apart when she was framed for embezzling from the family business. Now, with a chance to prove her innocence, will she survive long enough before someone tries to silence her forever?

Brant Law—FBI special agent. Brant selected Anita for the mission, but is far from trusting her. Before long, Brant wonders if she'll actually succeed in knocking down the walls around his heart.

Nick Tarasov—Member of the Special Designation Defense Unit. He trained the women for the mission.

David Moretti—The women's legal advisor.

Samantha Hanley, Carly Jones and Gina Torno—The other three members of SDDU.

Tsernyakov—Illegal weapons trader. He is among the five most wanted criminals in the world.

Philippe Cavanaugh—An international businessman who is up to his neck in dirty dealings.

William Bronten—Anita's old boyfriend.

Chapter One

She was bait, dressed in clingy red silk to attract the attention of every man in the room. The spaghetti-strap gown was sleek and sophisticated, the cut over her right leg revealing enough skin to be interesting but still acceptable for the serious businesswoman she was supposed to be.

"I've got visual of target number two," Gina's voice rasped through the nearly invisible transmitter in Anita's ear.

"I don't see him." She spoke under her breath toward the flower-pin-slash-microphone on her shoulder as she turned in a slow circle, her body tensing. "Where is he?"

"Upstairs to the left of the bar. Right under the chandelier."

She looked in that direction, but too many people were standing between her and the spot Gina had indicated. The lavish reception the Cayman

Islands Chamber of Commerce was throwing in honor of its members was in full swing, the black-and-white checkered marble tiles of the floor barely visible under the feet of guests who were networking, scoping out new deals and drinking copious amounts of champagne.

"I'm on it." She moved through the crowd to get closer to Philippe Cavanaugh, target number two.

Target number one, Jose Marquez, a high-ranking city official who had several retail shops on the island, had already left. But not before Gina had worked her charm on him and gotten a business card, along with a request for a presentation next week on what Savall, Ltd., the front for the women's covert operation, could do for his company.

One down, two more to go. They needed to get to all four of their targets. People were dying— the latest intelligence had linked Tsernyakov to the mine bombings in Africa. They needed results.

She made her way to her target without any obvious hurry, as if she were simply meandering through the crowd, maybe searching for a friend. "Excuse me. Thank you."

The air was thick with the smell of money— expensive perfume and exclusive cigars. Her four-inch heels clickety-clicked on the marble tiles, the sound barely audible over the ebb and flow of conversation that went on in a half-dozen different languages, the ringing of glasses being touched together, the sudden pearls of laughter that bubbled above the din.

She walked to the back of the gallery, through the glittering crowd. Philippe Cavanaugh, international shipping magnate, was where Gina had said he would be, handsome and debonair in his tuxedo, deep in conversation with another man and two lavishly dressed women. He had come, which hadn't been a certainty—although they'd had high hopes, given that the man was one of the main supporting members of the Chamber.

"I got him," she said under her breath and let herself relax. "Where are you?"

"Downstairs by the bathrooms."

That Gina would spot Cavanaugh first even though she was a lot farther from him and not even on the same floor, didn't come as a surprise. She seemed to have a special sense for these kinds of things, probably left over from her cop days.

Once Anita knew where to look in the giant room, she easily spotted her partner for the night. The cream-colored dress they had talked Gina into wearing looked striking on her petite figure.

The idea had been for the both of them to attract their targets' attention and the attention of other powerful men on the island—any of who might have had some kind of connection to Tsernyakov, an elusive weapons dealer who was at the top of a dozen most-wanted lists.

The relatively new piece of intelligence that Tsernyakov had a connection on the island was a closely guarded secret about a man considered to be one of the most dangerous men in the world. The task of finding this connection and, through him, getting a location on Tsernyakov was the seemingly impossible mission that Anita and Gina along with Carly and Sam—who were staking out the house of target number three tonight—had agreed to a few eventful weeks ago.

"Ready to make contact?" Gina asked.

A man walked by too close and was watching Anita, so she couldn't immediately respond.

He flashed an interested smile. "Hi."

She nodded to him, not wanting to be rude, but not wanting to encourage him at the moment.

"Are you here alone?" he asked.

"No, but I think I might have lost my date." She pretended to scan the crowd below. "There he is." She waved at no one in particular, then shrugged. "I don't think he sees me."

"If he could lose you, he doesn't deserve you."

His smile widened, showing sparkling white teeth. "Can I get you a drink? I'm Michael Lambert."

"Anita Caballo." She offered her hand and made a point to remember his name. "Thank you, but I think I might have had too much already."

"Then I'm definitely sticking around." He winked. "Besides, you can never have too much good champagne."

He was tall and sexy—dark hair, dark eyes— with more than a hint of naughty to him. In coloring and body type, he looked a little like Brant Law, the FBI agent who had gotten her into this mess, except for that battle-hardened edge on Law. Michael's infectious grin said his focus was heavily on *fun*. Nothing wrong with that. Law was entirely too stark and serious.

"Michael. Hey, Michael! Stop pestering the lovely lady for a minute and get over here. I found a buyer for your boat," a redheaded titan yelled toward them.

Michael held up his index finger to ask him for time. "I *would* like to sell that miserable boat," he told Anita with chagrin. "Promise you'll be here when I come back?"

"Promise," she lied to be rid of him.

He looked as if he only half believed her and

flashed another charming smile before walking away. She would have to have been dead not to appreciate the fine figure he cut. He probably put in his share of time on the golf and tennis courts at his country club. His compliments felt good. It had been a long time since— She cut off that unproductive train of thought and refocused on her mission. Michael Lambert wasn't why she was here.

She turned back toward Cavanaugh and lifted her right hand to her throat, worked the tiny button on the back of her ring with her thumb and took a couple of pictures with the microscopic camera she wore on her ring finger. Hopefully she got everyone who was with the man.

"You should probably move in before you get distracted again," Gina said. "You might trip over one of those men falling at your feet."

"Jealousy is a very unattractive emotion."

"Bite me," Gina responded with dripping cordiality.

"No thanks. I don't like bitter." Anita glanced toward the group where Michael was standing. He was showing the group pictures—wouldn't notice now if she slipped away, wouldn't follow and get in her way. "Gotta go."

She made her way toward Cavanaugh, one of

only five viable leads—four now, Alexeev had disappeared for good and was presumed dead—their team had been able to scare up after a month of hard work. And even those four… The evidence that tied them to Tsernyakov was circumstantial, at best.

She stopped when she was close enough to Cavanaugh to hear him.

"So he ran naked into the water, swam out to the closest boat and somehow got them to pick him up. Crazy, *n'est-ce pas?* But nobody can say that Monsieur Clavat is not a good sport."

His audience laughed with him.

She stepped forward and opened her mouth to speak but, before the small group could take notice of her, an interruption came from the other side. A short, stocky gentleman with bushy eyebrows pressed up against Cavanaugh and murmured something into his ear. Cavanaugh's smile turned grim for a second, then he pasted on a brand-new jovial expression.

"I apologize, I must step away for a minute. Work, it finds me everywhere," he said to his companions.

"You know what they say, there's no rest for the wicked." The taller of the two women threw him a look of open flirtation.

"And since I'm rather wicked, *ma chérie,*

there's hardly any rest for me at all," he responded with a knowing smile before turning and following the guy who'd come for him.

Picture. Anita remembered too late and was only able to get a shot of the other man from the back.

She opened her mouth to call out then snapped it shut again. Right now didn't seem like the right time to try to talk to Cavanaugh. He looked to be in a hurry. He might just brush her off. And she wanted to find out who the other man was, what he had said to put that look on Cavanaugh's face. She swiped a flute of champagne from a passing waiter and followed them at a distance that didn't seem necessary. The men were intent on their destination and never looked back as they hurried to the back of the gallery.

A hallway opened from the inconspicuous nook the men had disappeared into, partially obstructed by heavy, fringed curtains in crimson brocade. She waited a few seconds before stepping in. The hallway ran parallel to the gallery in a half circle, coming out on the other side. She was in time to see one of the tall, solid-wood doors that lined the walls close behind the men.

Now what? She strolled by, looked for cameras without being overtly obvious about it in case she was recorded, but found no evidence of security equipment.

All the doors had mottos painted above them in Latin. She passed *Fortior leone justus*. The just man is stronger than a lion. The sign above Cavanaugh's door said *Vincit omnia veritas*. Truth conquers all things.

She would have liked to think so but she knew, better than most, that real life didn't work like that. In her own life, truth had conquered nothing and it certainly hadn't set her free.

She listened by the door and discerned after a few moments that it wasn't going to get her anywhere. The thick wood blocked everything.

"Where have you gone?" Gina asked through the earpiece.

"In the back."

"Need me?"

"There's a curtained-off opening to a hallway. Let me know if someone's coming."

"Will do. Be careful."

Feeling better with Gina watching her back, Anita kept moving in case the men came back out. She didn't want to be caught loitering right in front of the door.

She needed to find a way to eavesdrop. She headed toward the next room as an idea occurred to her. All the windows were open downstairs to allow in the balmy night air. If the same were true for the upstairs, she might be able to listen in on what was said in Cavanaugh's room.

The sign above the door proclaimed, *Fortuna audenes juvat.* Fortune favors the bold.

Anita put her hand on the old-fashioned brass doorknob and took a deep breath, prepared with an excuse if there was anyone in there. The place was empty. And the windows *were* open. She didn't bother turning on the lights; enough moonlight filtered in through the giant windows.

She took off her shoes so her heels wouldn't click on the marble floor—pink marble up here to match the draperies and the frescos on the ceiling. The opulence of the building, which had been built during colonial times, was breathtaking on every level. She stopped near the window and focused on the low, deep voices of the men.

"Then *whambandot cor mantakna* yesterday…"

She pushed the hair back from her ears, but that didn't help any. The sounds were too muffled to make out individual words—or not enough of them to put together any meaning.

She thought of the old cup-to-the-wall trick she and her sister, Maria, used to spy on their brothers when they were kids, but a quick glance of the room didn't net anything the like. She pressed her ear to the silk wallpaper and curled a hand around it. Something of an improvement, but not enough.

She liked to think she was a resourceful woman. There had to be a way.

The room didn't have a balcony, but wrought-iron railings cupped the nearly floor-to-ceiling windows from the outside. They had a little bump-out on the bottom, six inches wide at most, just enough to hold some balcony boxes that overspilled with fragrant blooms she didn't recognize. She'd grown up in Maryland and wasn't familiar with the flora and fauna of the tropics.

She didn't want to step into the boxes—didn't want dirt on her feet that might be hard to explain away, didn't want to leave trampled flowers behind that someone might question later.

She grabbed the railing and placed one foot onto an ornamental scroll in the design. Flat, square bars would have been so much easier. She wished she were wearing anything else but a long gown. She focused all her attention on the task, balancing her weight as she leaned out over the moonlit garden.

Steady now. A tumble to the paved walkway below wasn't in the plans. *And I won't.* Not a good idea to be thinking about falling. *Focus on the task.* If the mission succeeded, she could erase the worst period of her life and heal the rift in her family, start new with a clean slate. To her, that was worth any risk.

"You can't get a building permit for that patch of land. I tried before. Environmental setbacks. Same as at Pirate's Cove," somebody was saying in the next room.

She could see a sliver of their window and the light spilling from it, but no one stood close enough to glimpse. Not altogether a bad thing, since that meant they couldn't see her, either. And in any case, she couldn't have spared a hand to take a picture. Balancing on the curves of the ironwork was tricky enough already.

Noise from the garden below caught her attention. A couple strolled by, holding crystal glasses, having a heated discussion in Italian. Anita held her breath, not daring to step down from the railing, fearing that one might catch the movement from the corner of an eye. She would have looked like a jumper as she was. She didn't need that kind of attention.

They stopped right under her window.

Diosmio.

The man fell silent. The woman kept on, breathlessly and with high emotion. Then the guy put his free arm around her waist and pulled her to him so suddenly that some of her champagne splashed from the glass. They were kissing the next second.

She felt a small pang of jealousy. When was the last time a man had touched her with so much passion?

"Zoning can be changed," the words came from the other room, drawing her attention.

Was that Cavanaugh?

Would the couple in the garden hear him and look up?

Probably not, she decided after a second. She could barely hear as close as she was. She didn't think the people below would catch anything but a low murmur, and even that would probably be drowned out by the general buzz of conversation filtering out from the downstairs windows that were much closer to them.

"I sure hope so, I'd hate to lose all that money," said yet another man next door.

How many of them were in there besides the two she had seen entering?

"Some guy is coming your way." Gina's voice sounded urgent in her ear.

Anita glanced toward the door. There were at least a dozen rooms opening off the hallway. What were the chances that whoever was coming would come into hers? She could hear doors open and close. Whoever it was, he was looking for someone. Probably one of Cavanaugh's friends coming late to the meeting.

She stepped off the balcony railing, anyway, just in case. And not a moment too soon. Her door opened slowly, revealing a dark silhouette.

"There you are. I thought I saw you come this way. Still alone?" Michael Lambert stepped into the path of the moonlight and strolled toward her with a satisfied smile.

She took a slow breath and willed her clamoring heart to slow. She could have been caught. "The cigar smoke was starting to bother me. I thought I would grab five minutes of fresh air and some quiet." She watched him. Was he buying it?

He smiled like a man who did, so she relaxed a little.

"May I just say that you're the most beautiful woman here tonight?" He stood in front of her, too close, and held her gaze. His eyes looked black in the dark.

She couldn't remember their real color from earlier.

"Thank you." She accepted the compliment that would have felt even better if he weren't interrupting her surveillance. Still, it had been a while since she'd been alone with a handsome man who found her desirable and told her so.

"So what do you do on the island? I detect a lovely accent from up north."

"Just started a new company, business consulting," she said, and gave a few sentences worth of details. You never knew who he could be connected to.

"Impressive," he said.

"And you?" Maybe she would recognize the company name. If he was ruining her eavesdropping, at least she could see if he might not be a possible link—maybe a way to get introduced to Cavanaugh.

"Land development," he said.

Any connection to the real-estate deal being discussed next door? "Sounds exciting." She smiled and tried to look fascinated. "Tell me more."

"Heaven forbid." He gave her another one of his sexy grins. "Boring a lovely lady is an unforgivable offense. Especially when there are so many other fascinating things we could talk about." He unleashed a slow grin. He was a charmer and he knew it.

"Such as?" She played along.

"I haven't seen you at one of these receptions before. Are you new to the island?"

"—going up." Gina was saying something at the same time as Michael talked, so Anita caught only part of it.

"Relatively," she told Michael. Didn't matter if they got caught now. It would look like they were up here with romantic intentions. She doubted anyone would bother with them. "You've been here long? I hardly know anyone here." Hint: I wouldn't mind some introductions.

"Hardly anyone is worth knowing," he murmured and leaned forward. "Present company excluded."

Before she knew what was happening, Michael was brushing his lips against hers. But despite how easy this could have been, her hands came up to his chest and pushed him away, even as her brain registered how nice it was to have that kind of human contact again.

Her heart beat a confused rhythm in her chest as the door opened behind her. Michael raised his head.

Busted, she thought and turned just in time to see Brant Law, FBI agent extraordinaire, walk into the room with a disapproving scowl on his face. He was a lawman through and through, right down to his stance—a perfect fit for his name.

He flipped on the lights and the sudden brilliance of the chandeliers forced her to squint. What on earth was *he* doing here?

"WOULD YOU LIKE to tour the facilities and see how the project is coming along, sir?" The man's voice was cutting in and out.

"No," Tsernyakov said into his phone. He had no desire to walk through a biohazard lab, to link himself in any way to this latest project or to break the anonymity of the assignment. "I'll be sending a representative."

"Yes, sir."

He hung up the phone and thought for a moment about whom to send. He didn't like for even his most trusted men to know too much, be involved in too many branches of the business. He kept them isolated from projects other than their own, from each other. He didn't want any of them to put together the big picture, to get any ideas about whether they might be able to take over from him.

He leaned back in his chair and ran down his list of top candidates, then settled on one. That should work fine.

A timid knock sounded on his door that he recognized as Alexandra's.

"Come on in, dear." He pulled himself straight and put a smile on his face.

"Is this a bad time?" She hesitated in the doorway, young and beautiful, unaware of how the pink T-shirt stretched across her breasts made him feel.

"You could never come at a bad time." He got up and went to her. "You look breathtaking as always."

She looked down and blushed. "I was wondering if I could go into town today."

"Of course, I'll tell my driver immediately." He turned toward his desk then stopped, pretending to hesitate. "Unless…"

"If you don't think it's—"

"No, no. I was just thinking that I had a busy day. I could use a little time away from the office. I've been meaning to take you shopping at Marks & Spencer. Of course, you probably don't feel like spending the afternoon with an old man like me."

"You are not old," she protested instantly.

"I'm not Ivan Ivanoff, either." Ivan, a famous Russian piano player about the same age as Tsernyakov, had recently married a model younger than Alexandra, the top news of TV stations around the country.

"No," she agreed. "You're much nicer. Do you ever think about remarrying?"

He shrugged and tried to look as modest as he could. "Who would have me, anyway?" he said before she could respond. "So shopping, then maybe a movie and dinner?"

"That would be really great."

Yes, it would be. He hadn't had the time to work on her lately, but tonight he would make sure she began to see him as something else than just a family friend. He put a hand on her shoulder. "I'm so glad you are here with me."

"Me, too." Her smile was genuine. "Thank you for keeping me safe."

"Nothing will happen to you, I swear." Not as long as she pleased him. That's what he had spared her for when he ordered the murder of her parents—something she knew nothing about.

He would end the year in style, with a new young lover and more money than he'd made on any one deal in his life before.

"Why don't you wait for me upstairs?" He ran a finger down Alexandra's face. "I have to make a few more calls then I'll be right there."

"Thank you." She gave him a spontaneous hug and was practically skipping on her way out of the room.

"Your next appointment is here, sir." His secretary's voice came through the intercom.

He glanced at his calendar. "Last one for today?" he asked to double-check. Sometimes people got scheduled in at the last minute.

"Yes, sir."

"Good." He would get through it fast. Alexandra was waiting.

BRANT LAW looked at Anita seated across the table, still not over the shock of how different she looked from when he had last seen her during their briefing at Quantico. She'd been a beautiful woman in the dark blue FBI training suit, but in this dress… Every man's head turned her way when she had walked through the restaurant's door.

Personally, he was into leggy blondes, but he could certainly see the attraction. He tipped his glass to his lips.

"Do you always drink decaf?" she asked.

"For the past week or so." He could hear the pain in his own voice. "I'm trying to kick a bothersome caffeine addiction." On doctor's orders. Since he had his hip injury, he hadn't been moving as much as he should have and his blood pressure had been inching up. He was determined to do whatever it took to pass his next physical. "It's all about discipline."

"How is it going?"

He groaned just as his stomach growled. "Excuse me."

Her full lips stretched into a sympathetic smile. "Missed your lunch?"

He nodded. He'd gotten into George Town on Grand Cayman Island late on one of those no-meal flights. His bad hip hurt from sitting still for so long. He wanted two things before he'd gone to bed for the night: a good dinner and a report from Anita Caballo on how the analysis of the financial records of their targets was going. So as soon as he'd dropped his suitcase at the hotel, he'd gone in search of her, concerned with what he might find.

Bribing four convicts to join an undercover team to bring down the king of all criminals didn't fill him with confidence about the operation's success. Could the four women succeed where professionals had failed? Carly was a top hacker, Sam a whiz at breaking and entering, Gina an ex-cop who'd done time for manslaughter, Anita a resourceful embezzler of four million dollars. Maybe they would have some kind of edge, a deeper understanding of criminal reasoning or whatever. Or maybe they were heading straight for disaster.

"How is the consulting business coming along?" he asked.

"Pretty well." She seemed to relax at his choice of subject. "We have a half-dozen clients and a couple of nibbles from others. Once we complete this first round of projects, I think we'll be getting a number of referrals."

Since Cavanaugh had left the party minutes after Brant had discovered Anita, they'd followed him to his compound on the beach. And as they weren't equipped for breaking and entering, he'd decided to end surveillance for the night and take her to the nearest restaurant that was still open, the Reef Street Inn. He didn't believe in wasting time.

She looked nervous.

Did she have a reason other than being caught with a man? Frankly, he would have preferred if she spent one hundred percent of her time and energy on the mission.

He chewed his beef—a steak and potatoes man through and through—and washed it down with some decaf soda. He poured some extra steak sauce on the next slice.

"I'm tempted to throw the poor thing a life jacket. You're drowning it," Anita said.

He made a point in sopping up as much sauce as possible. "Best invention since the cow."

She smiled and shook her head.

"So what have you been up to lately?" He didn't have a good handle on the woman yet and was impatient to learn more.

She gave him a detailed rundown on all the projects the team had put into place since they had arrived on the island.

He wasn't surprised that the business was doing well. She was a hell of a businesswoman—competent, resourceful, dedicated. He knew as much from her file. She had a fine track record with Pellegrino's, the company she had built from nothing before she had succumbed to temptation and neatly made four million dollars disappear. "And the other end of the business?" He was referring to the money laundering they did on the sly in order to get closer to a shadier clientele that could provide valuable leads to Tsernyakov.

"I wish things would roll faster," she said. "I was hoping to make contact with Cavanaugh tonight."

"Got sidetracked?" He drew up an eyebrow.

She shifted in her seat, but wouldn't look away. Good, the woman had chutzpah. She would need it on this mission.

"I was doing surveillance," she said.

So she was using the poor bastard. How far would she have been willing to go? He thought of her shoes discarded on the marble floor. "Is that what they're calling it these days?"

"I was trying to listen in on Cavanaugh's meeting next door."

"Find out anything?"

"Very little before I was interrupted. Cavanaugh is in some kind of a real-estate deal. He and a couple of friends of his are trying to rezone an area for building. They mentioned environmental setbacks and the possibility of losing a lot of money."

"They?"

She shook her head. "Don't have names. And I only saw one, other than Cavanaugh."

"Got pictures?"

"Not a good one. But I have pictures of others Cavanaugh had been talking to earlier in the evening."

"And your companion?"

"Michael Lambert, land developer."

"What are your plans with him?"

She looked like she would have liked to say, *none of your business,* but said instead, "None. I have no plans for him at all. He followed me when I followed Cavanaugh."

"Is he linked to him?"

"I don't know. Yet."

He nodded. "Find out." She obviously had no problem with cozying up to the guy. And Lambert had wanted badly whatever she'd been offering. Brant had seen the flash of anger and disappointment in the man's eyes when he had walked in and interrupted.

Was Anita looking for suspects, links to Cavanaugh and Tsernyakov, or was she looking for allies for her own purposes? Lambert had money, you could tell by looking at him. And with money came influence. Was Anita working him? Sure looked like it from where he was standing.

He didn't trust her, didn't trust any of the women, had argued against the mission and lost. He had accepted the assignment of working with the team—somebody with realistic expectations had to be involved—but he still thought it was nothing but an invitation to disaster.

You wanted to know how someone would act in the future, you looked at how he or she had acted in the past. By and large, past behavior predicted future behavior. What the hell were they doing conducting a mission based on criminals?

The way he'd seen Anita play Lambert tonight had left a bad taste in his mouth, an odd reaction since that was exactly what she'd been recruited for. And she had been good, he had to give her that. She had looked the part of a woman about to be seduced.

Anita, more so than the others, bore watching. She was the most beautiful of the four women on the team—dark hair, nearly black, cascading to her waist, the body of a dancer, legs that could mesmerize anyone. He was a sucker for high heels and she worked them like nobody he'd ever known. She was a lethal weapon even when armed with nothing but a smile. And he would just bet she was smart enough to know how to use what she had.

In addition to her intimate knowledge of financial wizardry, those looks had been responsible for getting her involved in the mission. He had picked her himself, from the list of possible candidates.

His attention lingered on her full lips, annoyed as the picture of Michael Lambert kissing her popped into his mind. What did he care?

Then all of a sudden his instincts prickled and he turned his focus to the rest of the room, scanning the tables one by one. Nobody was paying them special attention. Maybe he was just too tired and out of sorts. Still, he had learned to appreciate intuition over the years.

"How about if we have our food wrapped and take it back to my hotel?" he asked, unable to shake the feeling that they were being watched.

"What's wrong with here?" She didn't look comfortable with the suggestion.

He glanced around surreptitiously as he took a drink, and from the corner of his eye caught a dark shape at the window, the glint of metal. Instinct honed by years of conflicts in the field pushed him forward. He registered the surprised expression on Anita's face as he took her down, protecting her, softening her fall.

At the same time, the bottle of mineral water that had a split second ago been in front of her exploded all over their table, showering them with shards of glass from above.

Chapter Two

A woman screamed as people all around ducked for cover. With four years of federal prison and an intensive FBI crash course behind her, Anita managed to stay reasonably calm as she kept her head down.

"Unarmed?" Brant poked his head out, trying to see.

"Sorry." She had thought about bringing her gun to the Chamber of Commerce reception, but there hadn't been room to hide it under her slinky dress and her evening bag was barely sufficient to hold her cell phone, a tube of lipstick and the stack of business cards she had collected during the evening. She'd gone to the party to make connections, not to engage in a gunfight. She hadn't thought the weapon would be necessary.

He didn't chastise her for the lapse, but pushed her forward. "Let's go. Toward the kitchen."

All for getting out of there, she crawled under the tables among people who looked stunned, scared and confused. Spilled food and broken plates littered her path—a few tablecloths had been pulled down in the panic of the moment as people reacted on reflex.

Whispers came from everywhere, punctuated by a few sobs and some swearing. "Where did it come from?" "Is the shooter in here?" "Stay still."

"Stop moving around. You'll draw attention," an older gentleman snapped as Anita pushed by him, then fell silent as he looked at Brant behind her.

She nudged the swinging door open and slipped through into the hot and humid air of the kitchen, which smelled of frying onions and burning oil. She didn't rise until the metal door was closed behind them and even then she stayed in a crouch.

"This way." Brant headed to the back.

The man could move. The only two times she'd seen him before—at the Brighton Federal Correctional Institute in Maryland and at their briefing at Quantico, he seemed more the corporate type than law enforcement—crisp suit and calm, professional manners. But right this moment the FBI agent was clearly visible.

They passed kitchen staff huddled in groups,

some in the cover of refrigerators, others squatting behind the counter.

"Is there a shooter in the restaurant?" one of the cooks, a lanky Chinese man, asked, gripping his white apron with one hand and a meat cleaver in the other. At first glance he seemed prepared to protect the staff, but when Anita looked closer, his darting eyes said he was ready to run.

"Outside," Brant said. "Stay in here. Call the cops. Where is the back door?"

The man pointed with the cleaver, his arm jumping with nerves when a chair crashed behind them in the dining area.

Brant moved forward. "Let's get out of here."

Anita followed him down a narrow hall that led to cavernous storage rooms and stopped when he did at a door with peeling green paint on its wood panels. He paused a second then pushed the door open a few inches to survey the outside. Then he reached back to take her arm and pulled her behind him, into the deep shadows of the night.

The back alley was empty save the Dumpsters. She held her breath at the sour stench. Hundred-degree heat did nasty things to garbage.

"Come on." He strode to the street and looked in both directions before stepping out from the alley. He walked to the nearest car and had the door open and the motor started in under a minute. "Get in." The vehicle was in motion before she shut the door behind her.

"Did you see who it was?" She kept her eyes on the street.

"No. Are you hurt? Any of that glass hit you?"

She didn't feel any pain but looked down at her bare arms anyway. Other than being dirty from the crawling, they looked okay. "I'm fine."

"Call the others and put them on alert. Call Nick."

Nick Tarasov was special ops, the man who had trained the four-woman team at Quantico after their release from prison. He had come to the island with them right at the beginning to keep an eye on things.

"Have you heard from him yet?"

Brant shook his head. "He's only been gone for a day."

Nick was off to look for Xiau Lin, one of their four remaining suspects who was believed to be on a business trip in China. Marquez and Cavanaugh were on Grand Cayman. They had not been able to locate Ian McGraw so far.

Life at Savall, Ltd. had been relatively calm since Ettori had been shot—a revenge-obsessed hitman who had gone after Carly big-time because Savall had stolen a few of his boss's clients. After that danger had been taken care of, they had all felt it was safe for Nick to leave them for a while.

Obviously not.

She made the calls, reaching Sam and Carly first. Gina had just gotten in. She had stayed at the party after Anita had left with Law, to see if she could make some useful connections. Nick didn't pick up. He was probably stalking Lin. She left him a message.

"You think it's connected to Ettori?" she asked Brant when she was done with the calls and assured everyone that she was all right. She hadn't fully known until now how Carly had felt for those weeks when she had been under attack. "Maybe he didn't work alone."

"He had a driver that one time," Law said. He was referring to the kidnapping attempt Nick had stopped.

"Right. But that guy never entered the picture again. We assumed he was a one-time deal—a friend helping out."

"Don't assume." He pulled into the hotel parking garage and stopped the car as close to the elevators as possible. "Could be he took over Ettori's assignment."

"But Ettori only targeted Carly."

"Maybe Ettori's death upset the boss and now he wants all of you taken care of."

Not a happy thought. She got out and looked for anything suspicious, but the parking garage seemed deserted. Then she caught a glimpse of Brant and all she could do was stare. He was covering her, moving like she'd only seen people move in action flicks before: alert, gun drawn, ready for anything. Watchful energy and strength rolled off his body in waves. She could practically smell the testosterone.

He looked dangerous and capable and more than a little sexy, not that she was prepared to dwell on that.

The elevator dinged. She glanced down her dress, which was covered with food stains, and hoped they wouldn't run into any other guests. They didn't need any extra attention or questions from anyone.

They lucked out. The elevator opened on his floor in less than a minute without any incidents.

"This one." He pulled a key card from his pocket and opened the door, went in first, made sure the place was secure. "Okay." He locked the door behind them.

The room was spacious, the bed and armchairs covered in tropical prints that matched the curtains. She walked to the window to put some space between them, could see their dark office building across the street. She could even find their offices on the fifth floor, a little lower than Brant's room. Would he be able to see into her office during the day?

She was too nervous to sit, shaken by the attack, wary of the man whose presence filled the room. All of a sudden she had the ominous feeling like she had just walked into the lion's den. She looked around, feeling out of place. *What am I doing here?*

It might have seemed on the surface that they were on the same team, but that couldn't be further from the truth. He was using her to get to a dangerous criminal he wanted. She was using him and the resources he'd made available to clear her name. With little luck so far.

"Would you like a drink?" He was opening the minibar.

"Water would be fine." If she ever needed a clear head, it was now. Somebody was trying to kill her. "This is crazy."

"Did you expect it to be easy?" He watched her as he handed her the plastic bottle.

"I don't know. There hasn't been that much time to think about it. We've been going nonstop since we joined the team."

"And you've gotten some results."

She nodded. They had a list of possible links to Tsernyakov. That was something.

Her gaze fell on the suitcase by the window, a small carry-on. No other cases in sight. Didn't look like he'd planned on staying long. They hadn't expected him, at all. "What are you doing here, anyway?"

"Thought I'd check in, see how everything's going. I'm a hands-on kind of guy. And, of course, I can never pass up a chance to go someplace where there's even the remotest possibility of boating."

Naturalmente. And it was just a coincidence that he showed up the day Nick left.

"How long are you staying?"

"Until Nick gets back," he said.

He was here to check up on them. The thought made her mad, even knowing his mistrust was justified. She *was* pursuing her own agenda on the side. But that didn't mean that she was short-changing his. She'd given her word and she would keep it.

Here they were, risking their lives, doing whatever they could to bring his mission to success. The least they would have deserved was a vote of confidence. "You don't trust us." She was still jumpy from the shooting at the restaurant, full of nerves and unexamined emotion. It was easy to snap.

He was watching her, his mahogany eyes unblinking. "No," he said. "I don't."

The nerve he had. "You don't think we can do it, do you? Unwilling or incapable. Which one is it?"

He said nothing.

What did it matter? "Bottom line is, you don't think we have what it takes. And yet we are here. Which means you're risking our lives just so you can say you tried everything. I could have been shot and killed."

His expression turned dark. "Believe me, I'm well aware of that. And for the record, I never said I thought you couldn't do it."

"Just that you don't trust us." Her words slapped his back.

He drew up a dark eyebrow. "You want the truth?"

She nodded.

"I gave it to you. Now deal with it." His manner was brusque and hard, the attitude she imagined he used with suspects during his investigations.

Maybe she should go back to her apartment. She had been checking the whole way here—they hadn't been followed. She could call a cab at the front desk and be just fine.

As if he could read her thoughts, he stepped in front of her, solid as a construction barricade. "I'll take you home in the morning."

He was too close. She couldn't move forward and she wouldn't move back, despite the fact that he made her jumpy in a way Nick Tarasov, with his tough commando-guy stance, never did. Neither had Michael Lambert, even when he had his lips on hers.

Brant Law's mahogany eyes said he meant business. He was not a man to cross. She couldn't wait until he'd gone back to wherever he'd come from.

It would be better if he thought he had her full cooperation. She pasted on a smile. "Sounds good," she said, and turned from him. She would pick her battles.

"You take the bed." He went around her to the two armchairs by the wall and pushed them to face each other.

Was that where he planned to sleep? And was that a limp?

"Are you hurt?" He seemed such a wall of solid strength, it hadn't occurred to her that he could be.

"No." His response was quick, his voice sharper than necessary.

"Looks like you're limping."

"Trick of the light."

The light was perfectly fine as far as she could tell. What was his problem? This macho man didn't want anyone to know that he wasn't invincible?

"Okay. You're fine."

What did she care? She made herself relax, sat on the edge of the bed with her back to him and bent to take off her shoes, wrinkling her nose as her hair fell in front of her face. She reeked of cigar smoke from the Chamber of Commerce reception.

"Mind if I take a shower?" She glanced at him over her shoulder.

"Help yourself." He was digging through his suitcase. The next second, he tossed something large and white toward her.

A cotton undershirt, she recognized the thing as she caught it.

"You can't sleep in that." He nodded toward her soiled dress, without meeting her eyes.

"Thanks."

He bent back to the suitcase, pulled out a laptop and set it on the desk. Looked like he meant to work. She was more than willing to let him.

Shirt in hand, she retreated to the bathroom, into the bliss of privacy and the cascade of water, washed her hair, using up one full minibottle of shampoo and conditioner. She was drying herself when he knocked on the door.

"I called down for a courtesy kit for you."

She wrapped the towel tight around her body, opened the door and stood aside so she'd be covered and blindly reached a hand out. She pulled in the small plastic bag he placed in her palm then closed the door shut. "Thank you."

"I ordered room service, too."

Something to eat would be nice. All she'd had were a half-dozen microscopic hors d'oeuvres while scoping the crowd for Cavanaugh and Martinez at the party.

She unzipped the courtesy kit and looked at the comb, toothpaste, toothbrush and razor inside. She rubbed her arm where it was sore from when he'd taken her down, out of the way of the bullet.

He'd saved her life. He'd done so efficiently, with practiced ease, a true professional. And it just occurred to her that she hadn't even thanked him. She'd been too focused on figuring out why he was on the island and how much he would interfere with her private investigation.

"Thank you," she yelled through the door. "For everything."

"You're welcome. For everything." He sounded tired and distracted. He was probably on his laptop, checking e-mail messages.

He seemed sharply efficient while staying studiously detached. But then there were those acts of unexpected kindness, the shirt in her left hand, the small bag of essentials in the other, room service.

Brant Law wasn't an easy man to figure out.

HIS HIP THROBBED. It ticked him off. Brant walked into the George Town police department, using every ounce of will he had not to limp. He wasn't going to pass his next physical. This assignment would be his last. The thought left a bitter taste in his mouth.

All the more reason for him to want to succeed with this case, a big one, something to remember him by other than that one miserable, glaring mistake he had made five years ago. He needed this case. And he'd had to hand it over to a bunch of criminals. It was enough to put him into a permanent bad mood even without the pain.

"Brant Law, FBI." He flipped his badge to the man at the front desk. "I'm here for a consult. Mind if I get a cup of coffee first?"

The young cop looked at him, duly impressed by the badge. "Help yourself. It's in the back."

"Thanks."

"Yes, sir."

He headed down the narrow hall, turned at the end. Damn if the evidence room didn't conveniently have a sign on it. Locked. He looked around, produced his small tool kit, was inside the next minute. He riffled through the plastic bags in the in-box, found one with Reef Street Shooting scribbled on it along with the case number and date, then pocketed the bag with the lone bullet inside.

On the way to Savall, he stopped by a FedEx store and overnighted the evidence to his office for analysis.

"HOW DO YOU KNOW the bullet wasn't for you?" Gina was drilling Brant. She stood next to Anita's chair, Carly and Sam were engrossed in sorting printouts by the front desk. "What if you were the target?"

He'd thought about that last night when he couldn't sleep. The semi-sitting position the uncomfortable hotel armchairs allowed had been murder on his aching bones. And Anita's soft breathing, which should have been soothing really, tickled something inside him that wouldn't let him rest.

"The bottle it hit was right in front of Anita." The man had to be aiming straight for her chest. The muscles in Brant's jaw tightened. He was about to say something else when the mailman came through the front door, cutting him off.

The guy flashed an industrial spotlight of a smile around the room. "Hello, my lovelies." He stopped in midmotion and glanced around at the tense silence. "Came at a bad time?"

"Of course not." Anita, gracious as always, met him halfway and took the mail.

He gave Brant the once-over then threw Anita a questioning look. She shook her head with a barely repressed grin.

"Goodbye, then." He was pouting as he walked away.

Brant rubbed his hand over his face. He didn't even want to know what that was about.

"What do we know about the assault weapon?" Gina asked once the door was closed behind the guy.

"A nine millimeter handgun. I'll know more when the paperwork on the bullet comes back."

"Tsernyakov?" Gina threw out the name.

"That would be bad news all around." They weren't anywhere near Tsernyakov yet. If he had somehow been tipped off about the mission, the women would be sitting ducks. The safest thing to do would be to evacuate them as soon as possible. Which would end the mission.

Damn, but he didn't like that option. As little chance as he thought the women had of succeeding, he had no better ideas just now. They had put too many resources and too much effort into this to abort before seeing the operation to the end.

And they *had* made some progress. They had formed something that was beginning to resemble a team. They had identified a handful of possible links to their main target. If they could figure out who the true connection was to Tsernyakov they could get close enough to him maybe to get a location on the man, which would be more than any unit trusted with his capture had ever been able to accomplish.

Except, that now there was the extra complication of the shooter. Who was he? And what did he want?

"Any enemies?" He looked at Anita.

"Not that I'm aware of."

"How about your family? They know you're out, right?" Gina's and Anita's families had been told the women had been released and entered into some kind of rehabilitation program where they weren't allowed visitors for now. Carly and Sam had no close family who needed notification. "They must be ticked off over the money."

Anita looked uneasy as she glanced at the other women, then at him. "No," she said that too fast, as if wanting to close the subject.

What was the matter? Hadn't she told the others that she'd stolen from the family business? Pellegrino's was one of the largest construction companies in the state of Maryland, all of it family owned and operated. He watched her as she brought her expression under control. You wouldn't know that she was a thief by looking at her. Beautiful on the outside, treacherous on the inside. Now why did that sound familiar?

Probably because he'd gone down that road before.

"I have an off-site consult today," she said, probably looking for an excuse to leave.

"Cancel it."

"Could be the shooter was connected to Cavanaugh," Sam remarked from the reception desk. "Maybe someone connected to him picked up on Anita following him at that party or whatever."

Samantha Hanley, the youngest member of the team at twenty-one, wore nothing but black and had a fair number of facial piercings. Small scars around her eyebrows indicated that even now she was holding back for the sake of the professional image she was supposed to be projecting.

"Like Michael Lambert," Gina said.

"No, I don't think so." Anita shook her head.

Sam shrugged. "I mean, it's an option, but not likely. I think in that case someone would have caught her and questioned her. You know, like what she wanted, who she worked for kind of stuff. Probably wouldn't want to take her out without getting some explanation out of her first."

"Correct," Brant said. But he was going to look into it anyway. And he was definitely going to look into Michael Lambert. He had already sent off a request to his office for a full background check on the man.

"You stay put for now," he said to Anita.

"If we cancel work every time something happens, we will never catch Tsernyakov." Gina was watching him. "It's a dangerous mission. Stuff is going to keep happening. Right?"

Gina Torno was a tough one. He supposed she had had to be. Being a cop was no cakewalk and being an ex-cop in prison was downright hazardous to a person's health. But Gina had made it through—although, not without some scars.

She was right about the mission. He just hadn't expected something like assassination attempt to start happening this fast. First Carly and now Anita. Were the two connected? If not, it was a hell of a coincidence. And yet, as Gina had pointed out, they *were* working a risky case. Incidents were going to happen, dangerous incidents because they were entering increasingly dangerous situations. And that was exactly why they were here. He had known the score from day one. And so had they.

"I'll go with her," Gina offered.

He took a slow breath and considered that option. He would have preferred going with Anita himself, but if one of Tsernyakov's men was watching her, it wouldn't be smart for him to spend too much time with her, risking them identifying him. Tsernyakov had connections, "bought men," in just about every branch of law enforcement in every country that counted, the reason why they needed a team with a one-hundred-percent authentic criminal background, an unbreakable cover. "Okay," he said. "Be careful."

It was good for Anita and Gina to work together. The whole idea had been to forge the women into a team that could handle anything. He had to trust these two enough to let them head off to a business meeting in broad daylight.

He looked at Anita. "Mind if I use your office while you're gone?"

The look of panic that flashed across her face was quickly covered up with a forced smile.

"Of course. Let me gather up a few things for the meeting."

"I'll grab my bag," Gina said on her way out as she passed him.

He stayed and kept his eyes on Anita as she rummaged through the files on her desk. She wore a light suit that covered considerably more of her than the silk gown she'd worn the night before.

Her hair was pinned back. She had the tight look of business efficiency. He tried not to linger on her red stiletto sandals or her toes that were tipped with matching shiny red polish. She glanced up at him and smiled again, and he got the distinct feeling that she was playing for time, waiting for him to step out.

Not a chance, he thought as he willed his gaze not to return to her legs. Not a complete victory as his attention was now captured by her full lips. Man, he was a fool. Women always smiled the sweetest when they were trying to screw you over the worst.

HE HADN'T PLANNED on tossing her office, but once she was gone, the idea that something was off wouldn't leave him. He glanced through her files. Nothing jumped out. Nothing on her desk, either, or in her drawers. She was neat and orderly—that was about all the information he gained.

The space she created fit her. It even smelled like her—some exotic scent that included Caribbean fruit.

He plugged in his laptop and read through his e-mail, thought about asking Nick to scan through hers. Thinking of the devil, Nick Tarasov had forwarded some background info on Xiau Lin whom he still hadn't located, although he had found some

kind of a trail. Brant sent that file to the printer, but
nothing happened. Out of paper. He grabbed a
handful from the cardboard box under the desk and
refilled the tray. As he did so, the printer moved a
half an inch, revealing the corner of a dark blue
folder.

Damn. He pulled it out, looked at the shiny
new cover for a second or two without opening
it. She wouldn't have hid it unless she was doing
something she didn't want anyone to know about.

He wouldn't have minded being wrong about
Anita, but he wasn't surprised. She had betrayed
her family. And family should have been everything to her. It certainly was that to him. He
couldn't imagine any of his sisters doing something like she had.

He read through the papers inside, press re-
leases about Pellegrino's, about some of her family members who were now running the business:
her two brothers, her younger sister, her brother-
in-law. There were a couple of financial state-
ments, too, and other stuff—calculations.

On what?

Then it hit him.

She was, at the moment, the managing director
of a consulting firm that did money laundering on
the sly. If she hadn't before, now she sure knew

all about that subject. Hell, the FBI had trained her on it.

Brant slapped the folder shut and swore.

She was working on accessing the four million dollars she had embezzled and hidden and was getting ready to wash it squeaky clean. She was manning her own operation, probably thinking of skipping the second she had everything in hand.

Not if he had anything to say about it.

Chapter Three

She was out of prison.

He rubbed the headache at his temple. She was out and at the worst possible time. And she had lied. Whatever she was doing, this was not some government program to help her to readjust to society after her years of incarceration.

Where had she gotten the car from, the apartment and the job? He had expected some halfway house where he could get to her easily, where there'd be a bunch of other ex-cons and weapons and drugs, so when her body was found, not much would be questioned.

Instead, here she was in the Caribbean, as high and mighty as she had ever been, with another company and employees and money. What game was she playing?

And who was her guy? They'd left the party together, drove to the ritzy part of the island and parked. Probably making out. He should have taken care of her then and there. Maybe both of them. But it had been dark and to top it off the car had tinted windows. He didn't want to miss.

So he had waited until they were at the restaurant, all lit up, and he had missed anyway. And then they disappeared. He'd spent the rest of the night in front of her apartment, waiting for her to come home as anger and frustration boiled in his guts.

She wasn't going to let the last four years go. She would investigate, had started already, the alarms he had set in place had been going off one after the other.

He had to get to her before she got to him. It was as simple as that.

SAM WAS SLAPPING STAMPS on a stack of envelopes at the front desk as Anita walked in the door, back from her business meeting that was likely to net them another contract, but was—thank God— uneventful otherwise. No sign of the shooter from the night before.

Gina, who had reassured her that as far as she could tell they hadn't been watched or followed, passed her and went straight for the bathroom. They'd been circling the block for a parking place for nearly thirty minutes.

They needed to make contact with Cavanaugh. The weekly paper she had read in the car on the way back gave her an idea the other three women were likely to resist. Not that it would stop her from trying.

"The coffee vendor brought some flavored coffees and I made the Italian Delight. You've gotta try this," Sam said as she worked. "We're on our second pot."

The way she angled her head had a familiar slant to it and déjà vu hit Anita with a pang of homesickness so sharp it cut her off at the knees. She stopped and stood there, let it wash over her. *Diosmio,* how many times had she walked into her old office like that and been offered coffee by her sister? And Sam looked a little like Maria, too, around the eyes.

Was Maria still the first from the family to arrive to the office each morning? Dee, Anita's ex-secretary, had always come in late and left late, an arrangement she'd been happy to make for the single mother who needed the flextime to work around her babysitter's schedule. Dee worked for her brother, Rob, now.

Anita wondered if Dee was in love with him yet. Dee had the habit of falling in love with the men around her. Unfortunately, they tended to use her then discard her. She couldn't remember how many times this had happened since she'd known the young woman. But Dee dusted herself off each time then tried again. Some people accused her of being promiscuous for going after so many men. But Anita understood what was behind it all—a deep-seated, desperate need for love that she was always trying to find in all the wrong places.

Rob wouldn't take advantage of that. He simply wasn't that kind of guy. And Dee wasn't Rob's type, in any case.

Roberto, her oldest brother, handled safety at Pellegrino's. Maria, the youngest of the four siblings, did human resources. Nigel, Maria's husband, headed sales. Chris, the middle brother, just a year younger than Anita, worked IT. Anita had been responsible for the finance department. The rest of the directors were outsiders, hired for their skills, well paid and well appreciated, but the family definitely formed the driving force behind the business. They wanted to keep it like that for as long as possible.

On any given day, family members who were in the office would have coffee together in the morning, catching up before heading off to their individual departments. Pellegrino's was a beehive compared to Savall, the difference between an established company and a struggling new one.

Pellegrino's had more than two dozen employees in the office alone, in addition to the hundred or so construction workers and specialists they employed. They worked on several projects at a time, mostly residential. The hours were murder, but she wouldn't have traded her job for anything. Although, William, the last man she'd been semi-seriously seeing, had tried to talk her into quitting often enough. He'd been jealous of the time she'd spent at work. He never understood her—one of the reasons why they had broken up eventually. Still, the relationship hadn't been a complete wash. Her sister, Maria, met William's brother, Nigel, and the two were blissfully married to this day.

Nigel didn't resent the company like William had, instead, he became part of it. He understood that Pellegrino's meant family to them, especially to Anita.

She had built the company from her father's floundering contracting business. It had pulled them together, helped them economically and would benefit generations to come. Then someone had taken it away from her. The controversy that followed the conviction had just about broken her family apart.

The memories tightened her throat.

"You okay?" Sam was looking at her with concern.

"Yeah. Just thought of something." She broke out of the spell and moved forward. She had work to do if she wanted to get her family back.

"The coffee vendor brought all different creamers, too, and a new order sheet. We're supposed to pick what we want by Friday and fax it to him," Sam said.

She had changed a lot since they had been on the island. The imprint the streets and prison had left on her had begun to wear off. The resentful, sneering wildness had softened to a point where she could say things like "coffee is ready" without a snarky remark about whatever it was she chose to despise that day. She was changing her hair, too, letting the short black spikes grow out to a simple, straight do. Her original color, Irish red, put a smile on Anita's face every time she looked at it. One more cut and Sam would be a bona fide redhead.

She pushed the past from her mind and thought of that, of Sam changing and Carly and Gina softening toward the team, how they were now bordering on friendship, a shaky substitute for family, but the only thing they had and it hadn't been that bad lately. The progress they had made filled her with optimism and put the spring back into her step as she headed for her office.

The sight of Brant Law still sitting there with his

back to the door was enough to make her good mood evaporate. In the blue jeans and black polo shirt he had switched to this morning from last night's suit, he looked like a Ralph Lauren commercial.

"Hi." She stopped on the threshold. She'd been hoping he would be gone by the time she got back.

He turned around slowly.

Air caught in her lungs as her gaze dropped to the blue folder on his lap.

"Why don't you close the door, Anita?"

She took a deep breath and stepped inside, did as he asked. "I can explain."

"I'm sure you can." He tossed the folder onto the desk and flipped it open. "Trying to get to some pocket money?"

She had not said the words since her trial and fat good it had done for her there, but it sprung to her tongue now, pushed by some unreasonable hope that this time someone would believe her. "I'm innocent."

Shouldn't have said that, she thought immediately after. As much as she wanted to believe in it, truth didn't always triumph at the end. Why would he have faith in her when even some of her own family hadn't? Their turning against her cut deep, the wound still raw and open after four long years. "I'm innocent," she said again, and choked on the word that seemed to make Brant angry.

"I'm not the man to play that game with," he said, his voice clipped and cold. "You've done your time. I don't care what you do with that money when this mission is over. But while you are on this team, I expect one-hundred percent of your attention. Was there any confusion about that?"

If the door wasn't closed behind her she would have stepped back from the burning contempt in his gaze, but she was forced to stand her ground. "I didn't take the money. Someone had to have my ID and password. I'm just trying to figure out who it was. I didn't do anything."

"That was for the judge and jury to decide. And they decided," he said. "I've seen your file."

Did he mean her criminal file or the blue folder open on her desk? She didn't have a chance to ask.

"If this is not about figuring out a way to get to your stash... Why bother with trying to prove your innocence now?" he went on, his voice betraying that he didn't believe a word she had said. "Your sentence is up, you're free anyway."

She opened her mouth then clamped it shut again. She was not going to bring her family into this, not for a stranger. She was not going to drag out all their hurt and shame, would not betray to him the pain that still lived inside her and tortured her at night. To hell with what he thought. He probably wouldn't understand that even more than freedom, clearing her name mattered.

He was waiting on her with a raised eyebrow.

"I have nothing more to say to you."

"You were brought here to work a mission. That's what you agreed to." *Not that I expect someone like you to keep your word,* the look in his eyes said.

"I *am* working on the mission. We all are. We are risking our lives for it." Frustration strengthened her tone. "What do you know about any of us?"

He held her gaze. "More than you think."

Who did he think he was to stand in judgment over her? She felt her temper rise and welcomed it. She drew herself to a full height that wasn't all that impressive, but with him sitting, would do. "I have some work to do so this mission can move forward. Get out of my office." Then she added, "You want the truth? Here it is: I was wrongly convicted. I gave you the truth. Now deal with it."

He drew up a dark eyebrow and watched her without a word as he picked up her folder and his laptop. Then, slowly, he stood and walked to her until they were separated by only a few inches. "I'll be working out of my hotel room," he said in a low voice. "A word of warning, Anita. Whatever Nick let the four of you get away with, it's over. I'll be watching."

Then he sauntered away, leaving her staring after him, running through his words in her head. She was surprised he hadn't tacked, "there's a new sheriff in town" to the end.

"I CAN'T BELIEVE I'm wearing a bikini," Sam mumbled as the four women lay side by side on Seven Mile Beach.

"I can't believe I'm entering a beauty contest." Gina's voice brimmed with disgust. "Thank God nobody I ever knew could possibly turn up here."

"How do you know?" Carly asked idly.

"Cop salaries don't run to Caribbean vacations."

"I should take pictures. Some blackmail money could come in handy later," Sam mused.

She related differently to Gina than any of the others did. Carly had been intimidated by the ex-cop turned murderer, although she'd worked through that for the most part at this point. Anita had a hard time finding a connection with the woman. Sam, on the other hand, didn't seem to notice Gina's hard shell, which covered a full package of "dangerous." Could be Sam had spent enough time on the street to be immune.

"Keep in mind, kid," Gina was telling her now, "that I learned from the best how to make sure not to leave witnesses." But while her face was dead serious, she kept her tone light.

Joking.

That didn't happen often. But they had all changed in the last two months or so, let some defenses down, lightened up and some had even opened up. Carly had positively blossomed.

Had she changed with them? Anita thought. She couldn't see it. Maybe it was something a person could only notice about others.

Carly sat up and looked at the other contestants who were preening and slathering on makeup and hair products. One of them was sharing a small tube of hemorrhoid cream with her friend. According to the redhead, it reduced under-eye puffiness. Another was having a fit because a few strands in her bangs weren't falling at the exact angle she was trying to produce.

"I can feel brain cells dying just listening to this," Carly said with disgust and lay back down. "Participating might leave us with permanent damage."

"You said it." Gina turned her head as if it were too painful to watch.

Anita bit back a grin.

"What?" Sam was watching her.

"It's not that bad," she said.

"For you," Sam said, then pointed at Carly. "She's a nerd at heart. In the best possible meaning of the word," she added. "Gina and I are tomboys."

"What is this, kindergarten?" Gina drew up an eyebrow. "I think what you meant to say is that we kick ass."

"Right." Sam grinned. "Anyway, face it, Anita, you're the only girlie girl on the team."

"I'm not a girlie girl."

"You wear high heels when you don't have to." Carly seemed to agree.

"So what? I like heels and skirts and makeup. I like being a woman."

"So do we. We just don't like beauty pageants. Personally, I'm still not convinced I couldn't do more good to the mission back at my office with my laptop."

"Why am I not surprised, Carly?" Anita rolled her eyes. "You probably think the solutions to all the world's problems are buried someplace inside a computer."

"Well, duh." Carly nodded with a full dose of self-satisfaction as if she were a teacher who'd just led a not-particularly-bright student to the right conclusion. "Now you're getting some-where."

Anita gave up. "There are worse things we could be doing than hanging out on a gorgeous beach. Just have fun and go with it."

The Beach Beauty Pageant, advertised in *Cayman Weekly Entertainment Guide,* was open to anyone over eighteen who showed up at the announced location at the announced time and was willing to parade in a bikini on the hot sand.

Cavanaugh was one of the judges. He was everywhere, one of the most visible men in the island's business community. Would he do that if he had something to hide? Tsernyakov was so covert and mysterious. Would he do business with someone who was so out there? Everyone seemed to know Cavanaugh. Did that mean that he had nothing to conceal or that he was trying to hide in plain sight?

"I feel naked." Sam was lying on her stomach and looked stiff and uncomfortable.

Probably never owned a bikini before. Sam wouldn't talk about her life on the streets, but Anita could guess it hadn't been a bed of roses. "You look beautiful," she said. "I'm sure you'll wow the judges."

"Oh, yeah. I'm sure they're into bicolored hair, tattoos and pasty white skin."

The trouble wasn't white skin—they had all spent quality time with little plastic bottles the day before to get as fabulous a fake tan as possible. The trouble was with Sam's idea of self-worth, which was way off as a result of her past.

Nothing could change that in the next five minutes, although Anita was determined to try to help if she could in the long run. Right now, however, they needed a quick fix.

"Think of it as acting. Pretend. You walk that line and pretend you have the best tan, pretend that you're the most beautiful woman they are going to see today. This whole mission is all about pretending. Look at this as practice."

"I've been pretending my whole life." Sam's words had the ring of stark truth to them.

Anita swallowed the sadness that came over her, her heart going out to the young woman. She couldn't picture growing up without a family. Hers was large and boisterous, very traditional and fiercely loyal. They could love with a passion and hold a grudge with a passion. Which is why her conviction had split them in two. There were those who believed the presented evidence and the judge's ruling and those who didn't.

"One of us should get in, right?" Carly asked. She was good at keeping her focus on the project.

Anita looked toward the judges. "At least one."

The plan was that if any of them became a finalist—and would then be introduced to the judges—the lucky gal would bring up her workplace, Savall, to Cavanaugh and try her best to pique the man's interest. The trick was now to make it to the final. And Sam didn't stand much chance if she walked down the "runway" that was drawn into the sand looking all insecure and with her shoulders hunched. Anita glanced at the time on her cell phone and sat up.

"Better get ready. We have less than five minutes before lineup begins." She brushed some sand off her legs as she stood and tugged her hair into place. She normally wore it up or in a long braid down her back, but for this event Carly had convinced her to leave it loose. According to her, it looked more *smokin'* that way. It was also a pain in the behind, there being too much of it to be manageable.

"Good to go." Anita smiled at the other three, trying to look reassuring. "Ready?"

"As ready as I'll ever be," Carly said.

Gina nodded and plastered a smile on her face. She understood what undercover missions and role-playing were about.

Anita scanned the faces of the crowd that had gathered to watch the contest, looking for Brant and spotting him easily. He had promised to keep visual as well as radio contact. Each woman wore a necklace with a different medal that held micro transmitters; invisible earpieces were in place. They were unarmed at the moment, however. No place for a gun in a bikini. She felt pretty safe nevertheless. The area of the contest was cordoned off, special security in place. The governor himself was the guest of honor at the pageant.

Brant was protecting them from afar, watching for anyone suspicious in the crowd. More than the governor's security detail that surrounded them, Brant Law made her feel safe. She didn't have to like the man to admit that he was good at what he did.

They walked up to the forming line and found their spots. They'd already filled out the paperwork, received their numbers and had them pinned to their bikinis. Anita was first, then Gina, then Sam, then Carly; about fifteen women were in front of them. There were fifty-six contestants all together who would soon be whittled down to ten finalists.

They waited until the head of the jury, a well-built, blond Swedish-looking guy, welcomed the contestants and spectators, thanked the jury members, ran down the list of rules again and wished good luck and good fun to all. Then the first contestant, a wispy college girl in a white thong bikini walked down the runway, sashaying her twenty-something behind and Anita experienced a few moments of self-doubt not unlike Sam's. What was she doing here, competing with women ten years or more her junior?

She'd been thinking *mission,* she reminded herself, and pulled herself tall, missing her heels.

"Bravo. Bravo."

Number one got a nice applause from the spectators and gave up the runway to number two, an even younger girl with a Julia Roberts smile.

Anita watched the contestants go one by one, trying to figure out what the jury thought based on their facial expressions. The female jury members were evaluating in deep thought, watching through narrowed eyes, making notes. The men just grinned from ear to ear, none more enthusiastically than Cavanaugh.

Then it was her turn and suddenly the nerves returned. Deep breath. Confident. Think Latina pride. She almost had it when she spotted Brant behind the judges. Her composure faltered. *Don't look at him.* She relaxed her muscles and stepped forward. The twenty-yard walk—ten there and ten back—seemed the longest of her life. But she smiled and moved with the kind of easy fluidity that came from growing up salsa dancing.

She smiled at the judges, smiled at the crowd, in case the applause at the end influenced the votes. She caught a face she thought familiar— half a face—as the man was hidden behind the last row. But by the time she got back to the lineup and could turn around to look one more time, she could no longer spot him.

Nerves pulled her muscles tight all of a sudden. She bumped into the woman standing in front of her. "Sorry. I just got distracted. I think I saw an old friend," she said, knowing that Brant would pick up the information through the transmitter. "Hey," Anita said, scanning through the crowd again, "is that lady in the *back row* over there *on the hotel side* waving at you?"

"I don't think so," the body-sculpted brunette said, then went back to ignoring her.

Gina was walking toward the judges desk with the easy stride of an athlete, smile in place as if she had done this a hundred times before. *Nothing rattles that one. She's as tough as they come.*

Sam went next and Anita was more nervous for her than she'd been for herself. But Sam did a fine job and got a good applause from the onlookers. Cavanaugh looked decidedly taken. *Likes them young, does he?*

Carly strolled toward the judges, a tiny bit stiff, but it was barely noticeable. She was the tallest of the four of them, model material, not that she was aware of it. Her genuine, unstudied grace only added to her allure.

From the corner of her eye, Anita caught somebody watching her, felt the short hairs rise at her nape. But when she turned, she didn't see any familiar faces, nor did anyone seem to be staring at her in particular.

Diosmio, this whole thing was turning her paranoid. She shrugged off the odd feeling she was getting. She was in a bikini pageant, every man on the beach was here. Of course they were watching the contestants.

BRANT SCANNED the crowd as the head of the jury thanked all the contestants again then read the numbers of the finalists. Anita was in. He wasn't surprised. Then the judge went on to read Gina's number, then Carly's, then Sam's. Four out of four. They deserved it.

The finalists were invited to lunch with the judges, which was to start in an hour and the spectators were reminded that the final results would be announced and the Beach Beauty crowned during the beach party at seven o'clock that evening.

He watched the crowd and Anita alternately, knowing that if he could sneak a gun in despite the

Governor's security, then so could somebody else. The gathering was breaking up, everybody going about their business, heading for air-conditioning, no doubt. At close to eleven, the air was almost unbearably hot. He pulled back into the cover of the cabanas and waited for the women as they pulled beach dresses over their bikinis. If the judges had eyes, all four would be in the top four and Anita the Beach Beauty.

The thought stopped him cold. Where the hell had that come from? He was and always had been into blondes, probably a vestige of his younger years when he had a vintage Marilyn Monroe poster above his bed. He looked at Carly—she fit the bill. Didn't do much for him, oddly, which was just as well since these women were criminals in his care. He shouldn't even think about looking at any of them in any other way.

But Anita had something about her. Those dancer's legs and all that gorgeous hair and that superstrength steel inside her insanely feminine body. There was fire in her and plenty of it. Maybe he noticed her that way more so than the others because the first glimpse he'd had of her after arriving to the island had been in an intimate situation—with Lambert.

Michael Lambert. The background check on

the man had come back clean. Had he had contact with Anita since the party? He needed to ask.

He waited for them to pass him on their way back to the office where their changes of clothes waited, ready for lunch. They picked up their beach bags from one of the cabanas that fell outside of the security cordon. Now they were armed. He breathed a little easier.

Then he spotted some guy running after them and Brant's hand went to his back, to his gun. He waited. Maybe they left something on the beach. Or maybe he wanted a phone number from one of the women. Could be he was one of the organizers with some last-minute instruction.

The man slowed and glanced around. The row of cabanas blocked the contest area from sight and the people still around. Brant waited, his instincts prickling. He didn't want to make a rash move. He had to be sure. Then the guy reached to the back of his shorts.

"Hey!" Brant took off in a full run toward him even before he saw the gun.

As hoped, his sharp shout gained him the attention of the man as well as the women. The guy took off running into the maze of cabanas. Brant went after him, aware that the women fanned out and did the same.

Where the hell had he gone? Brant swore.

He hadn't wanted to start shooting, not with the governor's security detail this close. The four women were conducting a clandestine operation on the island, they sure as hell didn't need to come to anyone's attention. He would use his gun only if it was inevitable, only if he had no other options left.

Tires screeched ahead.

He abandoned the cabana jumble and ran toward the road.

"The fish market." Anita was there before him, pointing to the other side.

"Get back. Find cover with the others."

She gave him *the look*. "I don't think so. He was after me."

"I don't care." He was going into a dangerous situation and he preferred to go into it alone. Not only because instinct pushed to protect her, but also because he did not fully trust the women. He wasn't yet sure what they were about. Did he really want them armed behind his back?"

Anita wasn't giving him a choice. She was moving ahead already.

The fish market was deserted this time of the day, the air too hot to have food out. The flies were in full attendance, however, attracted by the overpowering smell. About a dozen rows of stands lined the market, each passage way thirty or forty yards long, most with roofs or sun umbrellas over the worn desks and empty crates.

Gina, Carly and Sam caught up with them and pulled their guns from their beach bags, went for different rows. They did seem to be working like a team, moving fast and well together, no hesitation in any of them. Nick must have given them a hell of a training in those two short weeks at Quantico. Regardless, he made sure to keep track of where they were.

He kept the closest eye on Anita. She was the one who'd been shot at the night before. Whoever the guy was, he was most likely here for her.

He heard a noise from behind to the left and spun around just in time to avoid a half a brick sailing toward his head. There were a lot of them lying around, holding down the stained tarps that covered some stands.

Somebody was moving low that way. The brick had been a distraction.

Brant crouched and crept forward.

A shot went off somewhere ahead of him. It hit wood, judging from the sound. They were all down now, in cover. He didn't want to call out to check if everyone was okay, didn't want to betray his location or the location of the women.

He stalked forward, careful not to make any noise.

To his right, a bamboo stick swayed along with the small wicker baskets hanging from it. He moved that way to check it out, closing in until the target was in sight.

The man whirled around and squeezed off a shot at him, but Brant was faster. He had the guy on the ground facedown, his right arm twisted behind his back until he dropped the gun. Brant put his knee into the guy's back to make sure he was secured.

"It's okay. He's disarmed," he called out and heard the women moving around as they were making their way in the direction of his voice. "Everyone okay?"

"Yes." The responses came in one after the other, from all four.

He let himself relax.

Anita got there first, which meant she'd been closest, which meant the bastard *had* been trying for her and not one of the others.

Police sirens came to life in the distance.

"Are you okay?" she asked Brant, then her concerned expression froze as he pulled the guy standing and got a look at his face.

Her eyes went wide and she stepped back. She seemed stunned as if the world had just spun with her, forcing her to struggle to regain her footing. The blood rushed out of her face, leaving her pale. "William?"

Chapter Four

"You know him?"

All Anita could do was stare at the man Brant was holding, disbelief and an overpowering sense of betrayal numbing her.

Sam and Carly came up behind her, then Gina, who stepped between Anita and William, keeping her gun out while she made sure the man was fully secured.

"Why?" Anita asked, finding her voice at last.

William shrugged without looking at her, his lips pressed tight. He was angry. He'd been angry at her before. For normal reasons. Right now he was mad because he hadn't succeeded in killing her.

The thought seemed utterly unreal and bizarre and just incomprehensible. "Why?"

"Let's get out of here." Brant pushed him toward the road. "I'm parked by the carousel."

"My car is closer. Next to the boat rental," Gina said.

The women had all come in her SUV, sticking together as much as they could since the shooting two nights before.

"Okay." Brant tucked his weapon out of sight then pulled his car keys from his pocket and tossed them to Carly. "You and Sam take my ride and follow us."

Gina linked her arm with William's on one side. Anita stepped up to do the same on the other, although touching him was the last thing she wanted to do. Sam and Carly walked casually in front of them, Brant brought up the rear.

William looked at her for the first time and tugged at her arm.

"Wouldn't try anything if I were you," Brant said from behind. "She's changed a lot since you two last met, whenever that was. My money would be on her."

William stopped, either because he believed Brant or because he accepted that he was clearly outnumbered.

Anita put one foot in front of the other, her mind reeling. The whole scene seemed so unreal, she half expected to wake and find it was all a dream.

They made the short walk to Gina's SUV in

silence. Sam and Carly waited for them to get in before they walked off to Brant's car.

Gina drove, William in the front passenger seat, Anita sitting behind Gina and Brant behind William, holding his gun to the seat from behind.

"If you have any doubts whatsoever whether I would really pull the trigger, do put your mind at ease. I wouldn't hesitate for a second," Brant said in a voice that sent chills down Anita's spine.

She sat in the back in shock, a million questions going through her head. How long had she known William? Six years, at least.

It had to be a mistake. Why would he do this to her?

The question grew to fill her head and push every other thought out. It had to do with the money. William had set her up and let her go to prison. The acute sense of betrayal left her body numb.

"Where to?" Gina asked after she paid for parking and pulled out into traffic.

"Go toward the industrial park." Brant grabbed his cell phone from his pocket.

She expected him to call Nick, but when he talked, it was in a foreign language she didn't recognize—kind of like French, but not exactly.

The car was slowing and Anita leaned to the middle to look through the windshield. There was a police block up ahead. Traffic was backed up for a hundred yards or so.

"Should I turn around?" Gina asked.

Brant thought for a second. "Take off your dress."

Gina stepped on the brake—they'd reached the end of the line—and did as he asked, but not without a disgusted grunt.

"Where is your number?" Brant asked.

"In my bag."

Anita reached for the bag—still stunned and confused and overwhelmed—and handed the wrinkled-up sheet of paper to Gina, along with the safety pin to attach it to her bikini. Then she took off her own dress and did the same, rolled down her window all the way. She understood what Brant wanted them to do—take the cops' attention from the men.

Get over it. Get over it now. Deal with the situation at hand. She leaned out the window and watched the proceedings at the head of the line. There were only five cars between them and the police. The first car was finally let go. The next held only a single woman. They let her pass after a cursory inspection. The car after that, with two young guys inside, got a more careful look. They even made the driver open up the trunk.

"If I were you, I wouldn't do anything to draw attention," Brant told William.

William didn't respond, just stared in front of him.

She wanted to reach over and shake him. She wanted answers.

Not here. Not with a police checkpoint just a few yards ahead. They all needed to remain calm, to preserve the careful equilibrium in the tension-filled car.

The next couple of minutes that it took to get to the head of the line were spent in silence.

"I'm sorry for the delay, but there'd been a disturbance at the beach earlier. Can I ask where you are headed?" The young cop who walked up to them was smiling at Gina. "You look like you are coming from the beach."

"Oh, my gosh, something happened? We were just there. We are both finalists!" Gina was squealing with excitement as she squirmed in her seat.

Squealing.

Gina.

Anita had to make sure the smile she had forced didn't falter when her chin hit her chest. She drew a deep breath. "We have to rush to get dressed in time for the big luncheon." If Gina could channel some overstimulated sorority girl then so could she. "Can you believe it?" She leaned forward a little and had the man's full attention. She didn't think he was even aware that there were two men in the car with the women.

"You better hurry. Good luck, ladies." He showed every tooth he had and then some as he waved them on.

Gina wasted no time.

"Well done," Law said, and she could swear he was smirking.

She gave him a cold glare as she pulled her dress back on.

He didn't seem to notice. "Let's get off the main roads." He gave Gina directions until they arrived at an abandoned furniture warehouse.

"Dock C." He pointed to the last loading dock then looked at Anita. "Would you mind opening the door for us?"

"Got a key?"

"I don't think it's locked."

She got out and ran across the gravel that crunched under the flip-flops she'd worn to the beach, glad to be out of the car. He was right. No padlock in sight. She pushed the rusty metal door in, cringing at the loud noise it made as it dragged on the concrete floor. Gina pulled in and brought the car to a halt. Brant got William out then pulled one of those plastic string cuffs from his pocket and tied the man's hands behind his back.

"You watch him for a second." He nodded toward Gina.

"You bet." She pulled her gun and stepped closer to William.

"Come with me?" Brant asked Anita.

She followed without argument, glad that he was taking charge. She was still too stunned to think. *Diosmio. William.* It had been William all along. She didn't seem to be able to get past the thought.

"Who the hell is he?" Brant asked when they were outside.

"William Bronter."

An eyebrow slid up Brant's forehead. "Related to Nigel Bronter, your brother-in-law?"

"His stepbrother."

Brant squinted his eyes as he considered her carefully. "What does he want from you?"

"Why aren't you asking him that?" She snapped. To Brant she was still the woman who stole a bunch of money from her family. She could see the wheels turning in his head and her shock switched over to anger. "He is not here to take revenge because I stole the family money if that's what you're thinking. He's not even in the business."

"That hadn't been my first thought," he said mildly. "How well do you know him?"

"And he wasn't my partner in crime, either." It hurt to have to defend herself again. Would anyone ever believe her?

"I didn't say he was. And I will question him, believe me. I just want the truth from you first so I'll have an easier time telling when he's lying."

The truth from her. Now he trusted her to tell him the truth?

"How well do you know him?" he asked again.

"Well." The heat of anger transferred into the heat of embarrassment.

"That well?" He drew up an eyebrow, a wealth of meaning in his mahogany eyes.

She nodded. No way around it. "We dated. My sister, Maria, and Nigel actually met through us."

"What happened?"

Diosmio. She hated pulling out more of her dirty laundry for the man. "We didn't want the same things." Please, God, let him leave it at that.

Of course, he wouldn't. "Meaning?"

"He wanted marriage and I didn't. I—" She paused, unsure how to explain it, not wanting to talk about it, at all. Had William done what he'd done to gain revenge? Had his pride been stung so bad that he would do anything to bring her low? Had he decided at some point during the past four years that it wasn't enough and if he couldn't have her nobody else should?

She hadn't thought he'd felt that kind of passion for her. Didn't that kind of thing only happen in South American soaps? Out of sheer boredom, she'd watched her share of them on the Hispanic channel in prison.

She needed time to think. She needed Brant to back off a little. "Who did you call from the car?"

"Friend of a friend. Didn't think it was a good idea to take this jerk back to the hotel."

She didn't want to get back to the subject of William. "What language was that?"

"Creole French." He looked slightly amused at her delay tactics. "Anything else you want to know?"

"Why do you know Creole French?"

"A couple of years ago I spent some time on assignment in Tahiti. Okay. My turn again."

He drilled her on a past she would have just as soon not relived right then and there, but did. He was just trying to figure out what was going on. She did want that.

Then he seemed to be done for now and turned from her, stepped away. A second later he turned back to her again. "Did this not wanting to marry the guy have anything to do with something specific or was it more about Miguel?"

The question hit her hard in the middle of her chest and radiated pain. "Miguel," she said, hating that he knew all this from some damn profile he had on her, dreading that he would want to pull all the long-buried details out of her now.

But all he said was, "Okay. Understandable." Then added with a shake of his head, "Good decision. Obviously."

She stared at him in surprise. The usual tough-guy mask of steel was off and he was just a man who in some way was relating to her. And it made her feel so uncomfortable she glanced away.

"Go get in the car," he said. "I'll send Gina out. You two get ready for your big lunch with Cavanaugh. I'll have a chat with William."

HE HATED TO BE WRONG. It grated on him. And he had been wrong about Anita Caballo. Brant played with his gun as he watched William Bronter squirm in the rickety wicker chair he had tied him to. "Was your brother in on this?"

William didn't respond. He hadn't, as a matter of fact, said a single word so far other than the occasional "Go to hell."

"How did you find out where she was?" He asked the next question although he had a fair idea of the answer. Anita had been investigating to find out who had set her up and had likely left a trail without knowing it.

And she *had* been set up, just as she'd claimed,

he was becoming more and more certain about that. Facts were: four million dollars were missing from the family business, Anita was investigating who had taken it and a family member had suddenly decided to take her out. Could be William Bronter didn't want her to find the truth.

And could be he wasn't working alone, Brant thought, hating to be here with the man and leaving Anita and the others unprotected. He would have to leave eventually, but he had to deal with William first. The man knew too much— where Anita was, that she was involved in something. If he talked, if the talk got to the wrong people...William Bronter was putting the whole mission in jeopardy.

"So let me understand you. You have the money. What's it to you that she's out? Why come after her now?" he asked although he could guess the answer. Anita was smart and William knew that sooner or later she would figure out who had set her up.

Bronter sneered at him.

Brant kept the cold rage that was gathering inside him under control. The bastard had set Anita up and let her serve time. Had it been revenge because she wouldn't marry him? Or had the whole courtship been bogus? Had he pretended it all just to get to her, to information that made the

Pellegrino's money accessible to him? "Start talking."

"Go to hell."

Brant got up and went over until they were nose to nose, dropped his voice an octave. "I've been there so many times I have a frequent-flier card, Mr. Bronter. Want to join me on a trip?"

ANITA STIFFENED at the knock on her door.

Gina stood, taking her gun from the table with her. "I'll get it."

"It's Brant," came a voice from the hallway.

Gina didn't tuck the gun away. She observed all caution as she opened the door and let him in, then locked up behind him.

"Where is he?" Anita asked.

"I sent him back to the States." Law sat, looking tired and frustrated. "He isn't talking."

"And you didn't want to push too hard." Gina went for her purse.

"Why not?" Anita snapped. William had set her up, had let her spend four years in prison, had split up her family. "I want answers."

"And you will get them. But I thought you might want him to stand trial for what he'd done. I didn't want to give any ammunition to his trial lawyers about how he'd been tortured in captivity." He looked at her.

The "tortured in captivity" part didn't sound all that bad, actually, but she did thrill at the thought of William standing trial. So Brant had held himself back on her account?

"I'll get going, if you don't mind," Gina said from the door.

Anita stood to lock it behind her. "Thanks for hanging out with me."

"No problem. Take it easy."

"You, too," she said, and went back to the kitchen table and Brant.

"How did the pageant go?"

"Sam took second place, Carly third." And weren't they both surprised to death. She grinned. "I'm sorry, I was too distracted to be all there. I think Gina threw her chance on purpose so she could come home with me and stick close."

"So Sam and Carly are with Cavanaugh?"

She nodded. "They stayed for the party to rub elbows with him. Gina thought we should come back and hang here until you figured out what was going on."

"Good thinking." He rubbed his hand over his face, looked up, held her gaze. "I owe you an apology." He was dead serious, unflinching.

"It's okay."

"No, it's not. You were innocent. I should have heard you out."

The acknowledgment felt so good it nearly brought tears to her eyes. She had waited four endless years to hear someone say this. She blinked, not wanting to seem utterly ridiculous by crying. She took a slow breath and forced a smile. "Thanks."

A moment of silence stretched between them.

"I'm glad I signed on to this mission," she said. "This way, I had you and the others watching my back. If I'd gone straight home, he would have probably gotten me before I knew what happened."

His voice was brusque when he spoke. "He didn't."

She nodded, unsure what to say.

"So I put a tail on Nigel." He leaned back in his chair.

She thought of her brother-in-law, a soft-spoken gentleman who put stars in her sister's eyes. "Did William say anything about—"

"No. Just as a precaution. And Nigel seems to be acting normal so far, going about his business."

"It wouldn't make any sense for him to be involved. He is part of the company. It would be like stealing from his kids." And it would break Maria's heart.

"They don't have kids yet."

"They're trying." Maria was among those in her family who had believed her without reservation and had kept in touch, so she knew what was going on with them. "He could have just borrowed the money if he needed it in a hurry. And he has money of his own."

"We'll see," he said, and cast a glance toward the pizza box on the counter.

She had insisted that Gina eat before leaving and had ordered it, not having the emotional energy, for once, to cook. The revelation about William had shook her to the core.

She watched Brant. He probably hadn't eaten since breakfast, either. Maybe, despite the formidable man that he was, he needed someone to look out for him, too, once in a while. "Would you like a slice of pizza? Zesty Caribbean."

He tried to hide his flinch. She tried to hide her smile.

"Don't tell me that's not your favorite."

"Pepperoni and onions," he said. "I'm a simple man."

Maybe when it came to food, but in every other respect, he was nothing if not complicated. She pushed away her chair and put the remaining four slices on an oven-safe plate to warm them up. She considered his job; his dedication to the mission; the way he'd handled the attack at the restaurant, saving her; how, despite the super-strong alpha type he was, he had humbled himself enough to admit that he'd been wrong about her and apologized for it. Brant Law was definitely not in the same zip code with simple.

He got up to wash his hands at the sink, brushing by her. And she was aware all of a sudden that they were alone in her apartment. A man who apologized when he was wrong and washed his hands before eating. He was almost too good to be true. She tried not to think of his eyes and his voice and that body he had on him. But she did notice the limp again. Maybe it became more pronounced when he was tired.

"So what's the story with your leg? Got injured in the line of duty? Did somebody shoot you?" she guessed. If he got to know every little detail about her personal life, then she should be entitled to a couple of questions, too.

He dried his hands on a paper towel, turned slowly, looked at her and paused. "Had to jump from a helicopter that couldn't set down. Hip injury."

"Recent?"

He shook his head grimly.

So the injury wasn't something that would get better with time. For someone in his occupation that had to be hard to deal with.

She put plates on the table then went to the fridge. "All I have is mineral water."

"That's fine."

She brought him a bottle then checked on the pizza. It had been warm so the few minutes in the oven had been enough to bring it back to hot.

"Dare I ask what's on it?" he asked when she slid the first slice onto the plate in front of him.

"Bite in. Live dangerously," she teased, deciding the mood in the kitchen could use some lightening.

He drew up a dark eyebrow, but said, "Not bad," after the first bite. "Spicy." Then he went ahead and polished off all four slices.

"I guess this means you find zesty Caribbean palatable." She looked pointedly at the empty pizza box.

"It's a complicated flavor."

"Meaning?"

He licked the corner of his mouth as he looked at her. "At the same time, more and less what I expected. In a good way. Makes you pay attention."

For a moment she could have sworn there was some kind of awareness between them, some unseen communication that had nothing to do with the food.

Then he looked away. When his gaze returned

to hers again, whatever she'd thought she'd seen in it earlier was gone. "Thanks. I needed this."

She gave him an I-told-you-so look.

His cell phone rang just as he picked up his empty plate and took it to the sink. "Go ahead," he told the caller, his face turning grimmer by the second as he listened.

"How did it happen?"

"Who was in charge?" He rubbed his hand over his face as he swore under his breath.

"Okay."

"Yeah. At this stage, I guess that's the best we can do."

Whatever the man on the other end of the line was telling him was making him very unhappy, that came through clear in his voice and body language as he paced the room.

Anita's stomach clenched as she waited for him to finish.

"Any other development in the case, you call me," he said, then clicked off the phone and turned to her.

"What happened?" she asked and when he didn't respond immediately she wondered if he would/ could tell her. "Was it about my case or Tsernya-kov? I have the right to know at least that much."

He came back, pulled his chair to face hers and sat down, leaned forward.

It was bad news. She fisted her hands and braced herself, stood up suddenly. "What is it?"

He looked up at her and when he spoke, he said the words softly. "While he was being taken back to the States, William Bronter hung himself in the airplane bathroom. He's dead."

Chapter Five

Brant saw the strength go out of her, even though she held her back ramrod straight, locking her knees so they wouldn't buckle.

"Take it easy," he said. "Are you okay?"

She nodded slowly, looking stunned.

No wonder. She'd had a few surprises lately.

The compulsion came, swift and strong, to comfort her, to offer her his strength, but it wasn't his place. In the end, he put an awkward hand on her shoulder, got frustrated at how unsatisfactory that was, then pulled it away.

"You barely had time to process that someone you once knew very well wanted to kill you. This is all just too much at once." He paced some then stopped.

She nodded without looking at him. "William is gone. We are not going to get any answers now, are we?"

"We'll get some answers. You have my word on that."

She attempted a feeble smile that turned his protective instincts up another notch. He hated seeing her miserable.

"You need a glass of water?" He stepped toward the sink.

She shook her head.

"Want to talk about him?"

"No."

Of course she didn't, certainly not with him. He'd spent most of his time since they'd met treating her like a criminal, discrediting every word she'd said.

"I could call someone over. Carly or Gina—"

"Not right now. Thanks. I just need a little time to deal with this."

Okay. *Want me to go?* That was probably the one question she would say yes to, but that was one question he wasn't going to ask, because no way was he going to leave her alone in the night.

"It's late." He glanced at his watch. Almost midnight. "You should go to bed."

"I don't think I could sleep." Her voice sounded hollow.

He knew how that was. You couldn't go from high action and trauma straight to slumber. There'd been plenty of heavy-duty days on the job when he'd been glad to be able to pass out by dawn.

"I can't stop thinking about him." She looked up at him again, moisture gathering in her cinnamon eyes. "Why would he do this to me?" .

"I'll check into it," he said, and pulled out his PDA, the best invention since ink and paper.

"You will?" She looked at him with so much gratitude it made him feel like a grade-A bastard.

Because his involvement in the case of William Bronter was only in small part to do with her needing answers. Mostly, he wanted to make sure Bronter had worked alone and if he hadn't, he wanted to make sure whoever else had been behind it all wouldn't interfere with the women's work.

The mission.

He had to keep his focus on that, had to keep her focus on it, hers and the others.

"Other than the folder, have you got anything else so far?"

She nodded, embarrassed, and went to the kitchen cabinets, pulled a large manila envelope from the top and placed it in front of him.

"You've been busy," he remarked.

"Sorry. I know I should have—"

He cut her off. "I would have done the same." He dropped the stack of printouts in front of him.

"Why don't you go lie down. Looks like I've got plenty of work right here for me. Might as well spend the night."

SHE STARED at the dark shadows on the ceiling, listening to the passing cars on the street below and the sounds of paper being shuffled in the kitchen.

William had come to kill her.

William was dead.

She didn't know which thought seemed the most unlikely. Then there was the string of "why's" swirling, playing ring-around-the-rosy in her head.

She had cared for William, had laughed at his wobbly jokes, had made love to him. They had turned out to be a good short-term match. He was a clerk at a major accounting firm. They had finance in common. She hadn't considered anything permanent, not with anyone since Miguel. She was scared of long term, scared of saying the words "till death do us part."

Yet, death did come, just the same.

William had been her second serious relationship. Not as serious as Miguel, though. They'd been married at nineteen and she lost him to a drive-by shooting the year after. She'd been in love blindly and fully with all the innocent enthusiasm only young age could produce.

After Miguel's death she'd run away to college, an all-girls school, as eighteenth-century widows locked themselves up in convents. She had wanted to be lost in work, to be away from everything that reminded her of him. She hadn't gone on one date the whole four years, then met a quiet, nonthreatening grad student when she was going for her MBA and they got together from time to time to work on assignments and ease each other's solitudes, give comfort of companionship and body. Love had never entered into the picture for either.

When she graduated, she'd gone home and took the small family business in hand and grew it with the same ferocious concentration she'd put into her grades. The intense hard work produced results. They bought a competing construction business, increased their equipment inventory, landed bigger and better paying jobs. Before she knew it, Pellegrino's had a reputation for being one of the best in the state.

Then, when the business no longer took a hundred percent of her time, William came waltzing in—all charm, amusing and gallant, knew just what to say, just what to do—and she let herself fall a little, holding back, always holding back enough so her heart couldn't ever be as badly broken as it had been after Miguel.

She never loved William, because she'd made up her mind from the very beginning that she wouldn't. Just as she'd decided that she would never get involved with a man who was a cop or a car racer or a pilot or whatever other dangerous occupations there were out there. She was not going to lose another man. If a relationship she was in ended, it would be because she ended it when she was good and ready.

Miguel had been a taxi driver. Picking up the wrong guy, at the wrong corner, at the wrong time.

Miguel had been dead for fourteen years and she wasn't sure she was over him yet. She let her pillow soak up the lone tear.

Miguel, the exact opposite of the FBI agent now sitting in her kitchen, guarding her sleep.

Brant Law was all battle-hardened experience with plenty of skepticism, where Miguel had been full of youthful innocence and optimism. For Miguel, everything had been about the family. She had a feeling that for Brant Law, everything was about the job. Miguel had given his heart trustingly, freely and with passion. She wondered if any woman had managed to touch Brant Law's heart yet.

What a fool she was lying here in the dark comparing the two. They had nothing to do with each other.

She had nothing to do with the man in her kitchen beyond the job at hand.

"How is the shooting affecting our business?" Tsernyakov scrolled through his e-mail as he talked on the phone to his Grand Cayman connection.

"My people are lying low. The police think it was probably something drug related, so they're rounding up the usual suspects. Because of all the publicity with the governor being so close, there are searches going on all over George Town."

"Meaning it could cost us money."

"In the short term, yes." The man sounded grim.

"Any idea what the shooting was really about?"

"Nobody seems to know. Word on the street is that maybe they were outsiders."

"I'm expecting our people on the police force to keep the heat off our interests on the island." It was a message he knew the man would deliver.

"They're nervous. The governor is demanding results."

Which meant that all bets were off. He had a half-dozen cops on his payroll on the island. They smoothed the way for the businesses he conducted through his varied channels. But when something like this hit and the police department was forced to defend itself from queries from above, it was every man for himself. The first priority of the weasels who took his money would be to cover their own asses.

And the cops were focusing on drugs. Damn. One of his ships was coming to port within the week.

"If they don't have the shooters within the next three days, we're going to have to handle it. I want the witch hunt over as soon as possible. Do we have anyone who hasn't been performing?"

"A couple of runners might be skimming off the top. I was going to take care of it this week."

"You take them and add whichever dirty cop forgets who's the boss."

"I'll set up a nice scene."

Yes, he would. The man was good at what he did. Tsernyakov switched to another e-mail account while he mulled that over. His man on the island would make it look like some fallout between a crooked cop and his drug-running buddies. The police commissioner would eat that up. He could report that the danger was over. The extra police activity would be called off. The governor would be pleased; the tourists who were responsible for seventy percent of the islands GDP could go back to relaxing and spending more money. He wanted everybody to be happy, for the status quo to be restored. He needed that for his business to run smoothly.

"I'm sending you something," he said as he opened an e-mail that contained four attachments. "The background checks on the Savall, Ltd. women are in."

"Are they good?"

Tsernyakov scanned the body of the message and grinned. "They told you they met in college?"

"Yes."

"The college of hard knocks. All four spent time in Brighton Federal Correctional Institute, Maryland." The more he found out about the enigmatic beauties, the more he liked them. From all accounts so far, they were beautiful, smart and dirty as hell. A nearly irresistible combination.

"What did they sit for?"

"Computer crimes, grand theft auto, embezzlement and manslaughter." He was smiling as he read the list that to anyone else might have sounded like a bad rap sheet, but to him was a damn fine résumé.

He forwarded the message, along with the attachments. "Let me know if you decide to do business with them." He wanted to know if they were as good as he thought they might be.

He liked the embezzlement part in particular,

the fact that the money had never been recovered. Smart. And instead of hiding with it and making a measly living, drawing a few hundred bucks a week so as to not garner attention, the woman leaves the country and sets up a business, makes a damn career for herself, recruits a team from among her prison buddies who are not afraid of a little dirty work. Attitude and imagination, not to mention sheer guts.

Maybe when he was done with Alexandra...

"If the island cops can't wrap the shooting within the next three days and you take care of it, make sure nothing connects back to you." *And through you, to me.* "Use someone new." A hired gun was never too hard to find.

"Will do. I have some business up north I was going to look in on anyway. If something must be done, I'll make sure I won't even be on the island."

"That would be best," Tsernyakov said. Being circumspect was a quality he deeply appreciated in any man.

This would be the worst possible time for anyone in his organization to mess up. He had too much on the line. His deal with The School Board was nearing completion.

ANITA LOOKED OVER the financial data Carly had gained on Cavanaugh so far. The figures definitely didn't add up. He had multiple sources of income so convoluted it had her head hurting. He was crooked. All the way. But beyond that, they needed to know if he truly was connected to Tsernyakov and, if he was, they had to find a way to use that connection to get closer to their main target.

She played with the business card Cavanaugh had given to Sam at the Beach Beauty Pageant. Sam had talked up Savall, Ltd. to the man. Anita had waited two whole days, not wanting to seem too eager. It was time to make the call. She pressed the numbers in quick succession.

"Mr. Cavanaugh's office. This is Linda. How may I help you?"

"Hi, Linda. My name is Anita Caballo. Could you please put me through to Mr. Cavanaugh?"

"I'm sorry, he's out of the office."

"Could you tell me when would be a good time to call back?"

"He left the island before I got in this morning and he hasn't checked in yet. I'm sure he'll be back in a day or two," Linda said.

"Flew out on his private jet this morning. The flight plan he filed with the airport specified Miami, Florida, as his destination." Carly read the information off the printout in her hand.

"Thanks." Brant leaned against the wall next to the small vending machine in the kitchenette. He'd been on his way over to the office on other business when Anita had called with the news. To Carly's credit, she had the information within five minutes of his arrival. "Let's assume that he's off on legitimate business and is coming back." As opposed to the possibility that they had done something to spook him.

"According to the secretary, it was an unexpected trip," Gina said. "Maybe he had an emergency."

"Family?" Sam asked, then blew her nose.

Gina shook her head. "The distant family he has live in France. Air France has straight flights from George Town. Why detour through Miami?"

"So he's having a business emergency," Carly said. "Found anything so far?" she asked Anita.

"No unusual activity in his accounts for the last few days. There's a lot of activity, but that's normal for him as far as I can tell." She looked strained and no wonder—she'd been through hell in the last couple of days.

"Okay, so whatever information we have on him so far, the number one priority for everyone is to go through it until we all know it by heart, see if we can find some connections." He pushed away from the wall, looked at Anita then at the others. "I'd like to add another item on our agenda."

"Nick found Xiau Lin?" Carly asked.

"Not yet," he said. "I've been looking into William Bronter. I don't like it."

Sam blew her nose again. "Sorry, hate this cold."

"You're not ready to close the case," Gina said with no trace of surprise in her voice.

"No." There were too many loose ends left. He would have to know why and how William Bronter had done what he'd done and where the money was before he could move on. Until then, there was still a chance that the case could be trouble again, interfering with their main mission. Brant was the kind of man who crossed his *t*'s and dotted his *i*'s.

"If anyone has spare time and wants to help with this, I would appreciate it." Gina could check the law-enforcement databases on Anita's family, Carly could get other data such as finances, Sam might help making some anonymous phone calls to check around.

"I'm on it. Actually, I looked around a little already," Gina said in her brisk unapologetic manner. "No prior record on anyone except Roberto Caballo. DUI when he was eighteen."

"He went through a wild phase," Anita said as she handed over the cup of hot tea she'd been making for Sam.

"Okay, so I was going to tell you this today," Carly looked at her and bit her lip. "I've been doing a little checking, too. It's probably nothing you don't know—"

She hesitated until Anita said, "Go ahead."

"I looked into the four people in positions at your family company to know how much money there was, where it was and how to get to it."

"Roberto, Christopher and Maria and Nigel," Anita said.

"And William, since we know for sure he was somehow involved."

"And you think he might have been working with somebody from my family?"

"Could be. He wasn't in the business. He didn't know your comings and goings enough to set you up. You two hadn't kept in touch."

"No." Anita closed her eyes for a second then opened them again. "So the logical accomplice would be Nigel. They were brothers."

Brant watched her. If there was an accomplice, she didn't want it to be her sister or one of her brothers. He understood.

"Nigel is having an affair. It's not the first." Carly started with the brother-in-law, her face reflecting just how sorry she was for having to be the bearer of bad news.

"He can't," Anita said, but her voice was anything but sure. Then she whispered, "Oh, Maria. This is going to break her heart."

"But the good news is—" Carly tried to force a bright expression onto her face, but didn't quite succeed "—Christopher is perfectly fine. As far as I can tell. No sign of trouble there." Her smile faltered.

"More bad news coming?" Anita asked.

Carly took a deep breath then blew it out. "Roberto was having marital problems around the time that the money disappeared. His wife had filed for divorce, then changed her mind a month later. They are still at some kind of an impasse as far as I can tell."

Anita nodded. "I knew they were going through a rough patch. But I can't see Carmen being bought. And I can't see Roberto giving her money to come back. He's proud to a fault." She looked at Carly. "What else?"

"Um, back to Maria—"

"Maria doesn't have secrets from me. From anyone. She could never keep one for more than a couple of hours. She talks a mile a minute."

"She might not know this one," Carly said as she drew a deep breath. "She was adopted."

The stunned look on Anita's face told Brant she hadn't known. Did her brothers? Did Maria? Were Maria's loyalties to the family perhaps divided?

"Any big money moving around for anyone around the time of the embezzlement?" he asked Carly.

"Nothing unusual. Nobody was in debt."

"Dig deeper," he said. Carly nodded. "And while we are waiting for a lead on this business, we will check out Cavanaugh's turf from a little closer."

Sam sniffled. She was coming down with a cold.

"You should go home and take care of yourself," Anita told her.

"I can do it," she protested as she drew herself straight and tried to look tough. "Superspy girls don't run from no puny cold."

And because she sounded like going was important to her, Brant nodded. "Fine. You go with Carly and Gina to the guy's turtle farm and watch for suspicious activity. Strictly observation, for now. Do not enter, do not interfere. Take as many pictures as you can—people, license plates, the layout of the farm, entries, any security you can see, whatever." She should be able to handle that even with diminished capacity.

"You're not coming?" Carly asked.

He shook his head. "Anita and I are going to stake out the Cavanaugh mansion."

Chapter Six

When they got to Cavanaugh's mansion, Brant slowed the car enough for a quick peek through the wrought-iron gate. He could see no activity beyond. The estate was surrounded by a six-foot tall stone fence on the street side and the property backed onto the water. Philippe Cavanaugh had his own private beach, with his own marina.

The Cayman Islands were a popular touchdown point for both drugs and illegal immigrants heading for the U.S. from South America. Did Cavanaugh traffic in either? His police record was pristine. He'd never been charged with anything.

Which meant he was as sly as a fox, because according to Carly, who'd culled his financial records, and Anita, who'd analyzed them, he had considerably more money coming in than his legal businesses produced.

Brant drove by Cavanaugh's mansion and the

next, pulling over at the corner of the street. "How about a walk?"

Anita unsnapped her seat belt. "Sounds like a good idea."

He went around and opened the door for her, held out his hand to help her from the car. Every movement she made was graceful as always. Her legs— He tried not to look at her legs. He'd never met another woman who could inspire respect and, well, *other thoughts,* in a man at the same time.

He had asked her to dress for a date and she had. Her sleeveless dress was made of some thin, silky material, tight on the top and flaring out from the waist to fall just above her knees, hugging her curves, flirty and feminine. Her high-heeled sandals— He drew his gaze up again and reminded himself that the date was pretend. It didn't come with the privileges of checking her out.

Man, this awareness of her that he couldn't shake left him feeling guilty and uncomfortable.

He took her hand and settled into a leisurely walk. The idea was to look like they were on a lovers' stroll instead of casing the neighborhood.

He couldn't remember the last time he'd been on a real date. He had a less-than-stellar track record with women. His most serious relationship—God, how long ago that had been—

ended when Jill had divorced him because she came to believe that he was married to his job and as she worded it, she didn't want to "live in bigamy."

She'd been wrong. He had wanted her, wanted the family they had planned. But he was at a point where he needed to solidly establish himself in his career. It wasn't going to always be like that. The hours he had kept were temporary. Jill hadn't believed him, wasn't willing to wait.

He'd seen others after that, but nobody stuck. Then came Lynette—lithe with big blue eyes and soft blond hair and looking, oh, so lost—who brought a man's protective instincts right out. He was investigating her husband's death. The department wanted to pin it on her. The first suspect was always the spouse, with good reason, plenty of statistics supported it. And Lynette had a juvenile record, sealed. She had stabbed her stepfather at seventeen.

She had told him her stepdaddy was doing vile things to her, broke down sobbing. Pretty little thing, so scared and shook up she still could barely say the words.

Then, that night, she had called him when someone was trying to break into her house. She had cried on his shoulder, wearing next to nothing. She had been roused from sleep by someone out to take her life, she'd said. She had put her broken heart right into his hands, telling him how her husband hadn't been the man others thought him to be, how he'd hurt her behind closed doors, how he'd kept lovers, had enemies, how he had denied her the thing she wanted the most—a child.

And when, toward morning, half-asleep from the exhaustion of a frightening night, she had pressed her soft lips against his, he didn't resist.

"I love this place," Anita said, making a visible effort to relax.

"Who wouldn't?" He looked up at millionaires' row and closed the door on the past.

"I meant the island. When we were growing up in Maryland—on the west side of the state, nowhere near the ocean—my grandmother was always talking about how it was when she was a kid. She grew up on a small island off of Campeche, Mexico. Her family was very poor and lived from the sea. I've never been to the Caribbean before this, but coming here was like coming home. I swear I remember the smell of the ocean. It smells different here than up north. And the water feels different, too."

He nodded, knowing exactly what she meant. It was a different world down here. He liked the atmosphere of the island—you could find excitement or peace depending on your mood. He liked the ocean, the relaxed attitude of the locals, the food. It would be nice if he had the time to go boating before he left.

They were reaching Cavanaugh's property so he crossed the street, pulling Anita with him. He didn't want either of them to be recorded by the security cameras that sat on the wall closing off his place from view.

A white sedan came up the street, stopped in front of the gate and was admitted in.

Brant paused and turned Anita so he would be facing the opening gate and she would be facing him. He tucked a long strand of hair behind her ear.

"Two men, early forties, suits, briefcase with the passenger," he said as if he were murmuring endearments to her. He also rattled off the license-plate number.

He lifted the hand on which she wore her camera ring and angled it to his lips to kiss the tips of her slim fingers, working the button to snap a few pictures. He wasn't sure how well they would come out, considering the lack of light and the fact that the gate was closing already, getting in the way.

He lingered, pulled the other hand up, too, playing the role out in case anyone was watching.

Her skin was soft, her hands graceful like the rest of her. He made a point not to enjoy holding them. It would have been grossly unprofessional.

But once the men had disappeared inside the house and there was nothing more to see, he couldn't help focusing his attention on the woman in front of him, on her upturned face and swirling cinnamon eyes. Her scent mingled with the scents of the balmy Caribbean night and became one with it. She was waiting for his cue, he realized a moment or so later. They should be moving on. Another second passed before he lowered her hands and did so.

"Do you think he came back without us knowing?" she asked.

"I don't think so. Carly is monitoring the airport logs." Although Carly *was* out at the turtle farm at the moment. Still, she had probably checked before she left. Even if Cavanaugh had filed a last-minute flight plan, he couldn't have gotten in from Miami already and be receiving visitors.

They walked slowly. He kept track of which properties had lights on and which didn't, especially those that were close to the Cavanaugh estate, out of habit.

"Do you believe in truth always triumphing at the end?" she asked out of the blue.

"I wouldn't be in this job if I didn't."

She accepted his response with a slow nod, a thoughtful expression on her face.

"How are you doing with all that information from this afternoon?" he asked.

She bent her head as she considered. "I suppose all families have secrets. Everybody just assumes that theirs is the exception," she said after a while. "How about your family? Do they have secrets?" She looked at him.

He didn't bring his family into his work, as a rule, didn't share anything about them even with his coworkers, but now, he said, "Probably. I have four sisters, all younger than me and unmarried. It's enough to turn a man gray."

She gave him a smile.

"Maybe William did work alone," he said, because he knew the idea that someone from her family could be involved bothered her. "We have no indication otherwise. Since he's been caught, there hasn't been another attempt." And, yet, his instincts prickled every time he tried to figure out the how's and the why's.

"Had his family been notified?" she asked.

"Not yet." He'd discussed the options at length with Tarasov and Moretti. "He'd told everyone he was going on a business trip. It won't be suspicious, yet, that he can't be reached for another day or two. He didn't have a steady girlfriend, didn't keep in daily touch with anyone according to his phone records. When he is reported as a missing person, the police will launch an investigation. I'll do what I can with my connections to drag it out."

"Nobody can know that he came down here after me. Nobody can know that I'm down here on a mission and not in some halfway house back in the States," she said. "If his story came to light it would compromise the mission."

"Right."

"Diosmio." She shook her head. "From federal prison straight into a undercover operation that now involves a government cover-up of the death of a suspect in custody. My career is moving up."

They walked in silence for a while, reached the end of the street and turned around. And suddenly they were just walking along as any other couple on a moonlit, romantic night.

He glanced through Cavanaugh's gate when they reached it again. Nothing new in there. They had to keep on going. When they got to the car, he opened the door for her.

"Thanks."

He went around and took his own place.

Silence filled the small space as they both kept their eyes on the rearview mirror. What was she thinking about? He didn't want things to start feeling awkward so he asked, "What are you going to do first when you get home?"

Just as she asked, "Hungry?"

"Kiss my nieces and nephews senseless," she said.

"Yeah," he responded to her question.

She pulled her black leather purse, which looked like a small backpack, from the backseat, brushing against his arm on her way back. His awareness of her was becoming pitiful.

She produced two cans of soda along with plastic-wrapped sandwiches. "Help yourself, there's more."

"Thanks." He unwrapped a sandwich and bit in. The explosion of flavors surprised him. He opened his sandwich and peered in. "What's that?"

"Salsa. You don't like it?"

He just hadn't known he did. "It's great," he said, shifting in his seat. His hip had been hurting almost constantly for the last couple of days. Maybe bad weather was coming—hurricane season and all. The thought was depressing. You knew you were getting old when you got your weather forecast from your bones instead of the evening news.

"Are you okay?" Anita asked.

She had a sixth sense to notice whenever anything was wrong with anyone. He'd seen it at work at the office. She always looked out for the others.

"Nothing serious," he said, tired of denying the problem.

"You're worried that it'll affect your work," she said.

"It'll end my work." It felt liberating to say the words, at last.

"That must be hard to accept."

He thought for a moment. It should have been hard to accept, but it wasn't. He shook his head. "I think I'm ready." He had seen enough, had been on enough hair-raising cases to be okay with calling it quits. And despite what his ex, Jill, had thought, family did come before the job. And he wanted one. Maybe if he settled down, his wayward sisters would follow his example.

He considered Eileen Mills, one of his neighbors back in Virginia, a sweet-natured schoolteacher who sometimes brought over oatmeal-raisin cookies, the best he'd ever tasted. She was sweet and kind and caring, the type of woman a man could envision raising his children.

They were friends, had been friends for years, which he considered a good foundation for marriage. He had thought about taking their relationship to the next level a couple times over the past year, but never got around to it. After this mission, he would have plenty of time to woo her. He didn't have time to think about her right now.

Movement in the rearview mirror caught his eye. The white sedan was leaving.

"Put your head on my shoulder," he told Anita.

She did so without hesitation. He took her hand and pulled it to him again, not to take pictures, just to round out the image they presented.

She fit into the crook of his neck perfectly. The way she felt pressed against him— A better man wouldn't notice stuff like that, but he was obviously scum because he was aware of every inch of her body that touched his.

She was off-limits. Nothing was going to happen between them. She wasn't his type anyway.

Tell yourself that a few hundred times, pal, and see if you start believing it.

The car went by them, stopped then rolled out into the cross street.

"We're not following them?" she asked.

"Not necessary. I got the plate numbers. We'll know who they are by tomorrow."

She was pulling away when a cop car came up behind them. Parked.

He watched in his side mirror as a female officer got out. Probably one of the neighbors had reported them. Neighborhoods like this didn't like outsiders hanging around.

"Damn. We don't need to get on the radar of the local police."

"What does she want? We haven't done anything wrong."

"Let's hope she doesn't get it into her head that we're would-be burglars. The car is full of surveillance equipment." He pushed his night-vision binoculars deep under his seat with the heel of his right shoe.

"She can't just search the car, can she?" Anita glanced into the rearview mirror.

"It's not the U.S. She can probably do anything she wants."

"Good evening," the policewoman said as she came up to his rolled down window.

"Good evening, officer."

"Are you having any problems?" she asked.

"Just talking," he said.

She bent to get a better look at Anita, then at him again, drew her own conclusions as to why a man and a woman would sit on a secluded street when they wanted to spend time together instead of walking the public beaches or going to one of the many restaurants or back to one of their apartments, for that matter. Her voice was crisp as she said, "Go home to your wife, sir." And walked away.

He glanced at the clock on the dashboard. It was

half past midnight. The windows at the Cavanaugh estate had gone dark, everything quiet. He turned the key in the ignition and pulled away from the curb.

Time to check in with Gina, Carly and Sam. Maybe they'd had better luck.

HE COULDN'T get her home fast enough, Anita thought, embarrassed by her body's reaction to him in the close confines of the car. The evening had been probably no big deal to him but it had been four years since she'd been out with a man, held hands, touched bodies—even if tonight was just pretend. Brant Law kissing her fingertips filled her with more heat than biting into a chili pepper.

"I'll walk you up," he said when he stopped the car in front of her apartment building.

"It's not necessary." His hip was hurting and her apartment building had no elevator. It wasn't tall enough to require one, she supposed. She lived on the third floor, the very top.

"Just the same," he said, and got out, managing to get over to her side fast enough to open the door for her.

The walk up the stairs was silent and awkward. Then again, maybe she was just projecting her frazzled frame of mind onto him. She was glad when they made it to her door. She pushed the key in the lock.

"I'll go first." He stepped forward and pushed the door open slowly with his left hand while his right hovered over the gun tucked into the back of his jeans. She waited a few seconds before she followed him in.

He held a hand up to signal her to stop where she was.

He was probably overdoing it, but she couldn't be mad at him for it. She was thorough—a quality they shared. She also believed in doing a job well and leaving it fully finished.

She glanced around and her attention caught the stack of papers she had left on the kitchen counter. Something wasn't right about them. A plastic bag was shut in the door of a cabinet above the stove.

"Somebody was in here," she called out.

"Don't touch anything," came the response from her bedroom, then Brant appeared a second later. "Whoever it was, he's gone now. I'll come back with a fingerprint kit tomorrow. We'll get you a room at my hotel for tonight," he said.

Anita backed out into the hallway. Sticking close to him was probably the smart thing to do. But she really, really needed distance right now.

"I could crash with one of the other women. Sam is sick. She needs a little caring, anyway."

"Not when there's someone after you," he said.

He was right. She didn't want to bring danger to anyone. She wasn't thinking straight. "Okay." A room at the other end of the hotel should be fine. And she was not going over to visit with him under any circumstances. Seriously. Sooner or later he was going to catch onto the effect he was having on her and she was going to end up making a fool out of herself.

But not tonight.

HE HADN'T TOSSED her courtesy kit. She'd forgotten to do so before she left, frazzled by having spent the night in his room. It still sat there on the bathroom sink.

She knew this because the hotel had been booked full. They were roommates again.

Anita brushed her teeth and combed her hair, looked at herself in the mirror. He'd given her a shirt to sleep in once again. The hem came nearly to her knees. It didn't stop her from feeling naked.

She came out of the bathroom with some reluctance. "All yours."

"Thanks," he said as he passed by her on his way in.

Their eyes met. Her mouth went powder dry and she licked her lips, needing to say something to diffuse the situation, but it was he who broke the spell.

"Gina called in. Their stakeout was a wash. 'Nothing but thousands of humping turtles and an ungodly stench' were the exact words." A smile played above his lips.

"Sounds like we got the better end of the deal." She tried, in vain, to make herself relax.

Once the door was closed behind him, she walked over and collapsed on the bed. *Diosmio*. Her nerve endings were still tingling. It made no sense to be this shaken up because they were sharing a room. They'd done so before. And besides, these weren't nearly as cramped quarters as the car they'd spent the first half of the night in.

She glanced at the turned armchairs he had obviously planned to sleep in again. She pulled a pillow and a blanket from the bed, made up the chairs and settled in, turned on the TV and flipped through the channels, settling on the local news. She needed distraction. Peace. Serenity. Anything to keep from thinking about Brant.

But then the water started up in the bathroom and the domestic mood of the scene hit her with full force, leaving her unable to concentrate on what the anchorwoman was saying. Life could be like this. Again.

She'd had that before, a home and a man who loved her to share it with. There was a fierce longing in her that went beyond the loss of Miguel. She wanted this again, she realized. She wanted a partner, a mate. She'd done the grieving. She'd done the career thing and the building of the business. She'd done the self-examination and the loneliness. She'd thought she would be happy just to have her freedom and her family back. She'd been wrong. She wanted moonlit walks. She wanted love. God help her, she wanted a man in her shower.

When the bathroom door opened, she didn't look over. She was afraid Brant would see the bare-naked need in her eyes.

He came up to her and, judging from the sound, he was still rubbing a towel over his head. Out of the corner of her eye she saw that he was wearing a pair of shorts with an elastic waistband, the kind people wore to go running or play soccer. "You take the bed," he said.

"It's okay."

"Anita."

She had to look up at him. "Let's take turns. I got it last time."

He just stood there, looking ridiculously strong and maddeningly unmovable.

"Your hip—"

"Will be fine. You don't need to mother me like you do the others at the office."

Nothing could have been further from her thoughts than mothering him as she took in his naked chest and the drops of water that glistened on the sparse smattering of hair. She pulled up her gaze to his.

Did the heat she saw there come from her own wishful thinking?

She needed to put distance between them before she said or did something stupid. And since he wasn't moving, she had to. She swung her legs to the floor and stood up, meaning to make a beeline for the bed, but her legs didn't seem to obey her once they were standing toe to toe.

He dropped the damp towel on the carpet at the foot of the chair. His hands, warm and strong, came up to her face and cupped her with tenderness.

He smelled clean fresh, the citrus scent of the hotel soap on his skin, the minty scent of toothpaste, the man himself. He was the kind of man a woman could lose herself to, heart and soul. The thought scared her and thrilled her at the same time.

She let her eyes drift closed and gave herself up to the kiss she knew was inevitably coming.

He let her go abruptly and stepped away, put some four feet of distance between them.

"I apologize. I was out of line." His voice sounded rusty.

"It's fine," she said, cringing, as she walked to the bed and escaped under the covers.

"And we have some breaking news coming in. Acting on an anonymous tip in connection with Wednesday's shooting, island police swarmed a condominium complex on Sunset Parkway today." The television drew her attention.

"They arrived just hours after an apparent shoot-out that left two men dead. They were identified as police officer Richard Mayen and Louis Marceau, a French citizen with a previous arrest record in Haiti. Documents as well as a considerable amount of cash and drugs in the apartment indicate that the shooting was most likely drug related. An official statement from the chief of police will be released at 6:00 a.m. We will, of course, cover the event live. It is expected, however, that this will end the investigation into the Wednesday shooting that had drawn attention because of its proximity to the governor." The anchorwoman went on, but the rest of what she was saying was little

more than an advertising for their early morning forecast.

"So Mayen was a dirty cop. The fish-market shooting case will be closed."

"He could have worked for anyone. Anonymous call, incriminating documents— Case sounds a little too pat, doesn't it?" His eyes narrowed as he considered. "It has cover-up stamped all over it."

She sat up. "We did the shooting. I mean, William. Why would anybody on the island want to cover for him?"

"Who even knows that he was involved?" He tapped his feet.

"Had William been allowed any contact after you took him?" she asked.

He shook his head. "We figured he'd have plenty of time to lawyer up once we got him back to the States."

"You don't think this was done by your people?" She gestured toward the television. According to Nick, even the U.S. government sometimes worked with assassins.

"No." He sounded very sure of himself.

With good reason, she supposed. On this operation, he was the boss. He would know.

"So, it's good news, right?" she asked, considering all the obvious implications. "At least the police won't be sniffing around after us."

"I would have preferred the police. I don't like the idea of some unknown entity who seems to know our business," he said.

Chapter Seven

Brant opened the door for her. She liked that, his old-fashioned manners. Common courtesy was all too rare these days.

"We got Ian McGraw." Carly greeted them as they stepped into the office.

"So where is he?" Anita asked.

"In rehab."

Brant's eyebrows slid up his face. "For how long?"

"No way to tell. He's got a nasty meth addiction going. He checked in a month ago."

About the time the women had arrived on the island.

"Doesn't mean he's not our man," Anita said.

"But makes it unlikely. Tsernyakov is not stupid. He has his associates checked out. He wouldn't trust his business to someone who is unstable."

That sounded logical. "So we are down to three: Marquez, Cavanaugh and Lin."

"Can't do anything about Lin until he returns to the island. Let's get working on the double on eliminating or confirming the other two."

"I forwarded you some more financial records, Anita," Carly said.

"Thanks." She walked toward her office. "I'll get right on it."

She tossed down her bag and turned on her PC, ready to work.

Brant stopped by her office, his wide shoulders nearly filling the doorway. Anita turned to her computer screen. She was not going to notice any more things like that about him.

"Let me know as soon as you have anything," he said before he walked away.

I have something, all right, she thought—an impossible crush on an FBI agent who probably sees me as nothing more than a means to get to Tsernyakov.

She couldn't think about him like that, just couldn't. She had people trying to kill her while she was going after one of the most dangerous criminals on the planet. She had a life to rebuild. She couldn't afford to waste time on flights of fancy. Brant Law fell into the realm of the un-reachable and impossible as far as she was concerned. She would do herself a favor to remember that.

"How soon do you need the space?" Cal was asking.

Tsernyakov looked at the cousin whose warehousing business in England he'd just saved with his connections. "Maybe as soon as next week. Can you help?"

"Whatever it takes, I'm going to make it happen. I can't tell you how grateful I am for what you've done for me."

His straight patrician nose reminded Tsernyakov of his aunt, Irina. So far he liked the boy. "It was nothing," he said modestly. "We are family."

"If there is anything I can do for you, now or anytime in the future, consider it done."

"I appreciate that, but I really wouldn't want to take advantage. It's just that this thing has come up suddenly and it's good business. I don't want to miss out. You know how it can be sometimes."

"You find a good deal, you need to grab it before somebody else does."

"Right. You're a businessman, yourself. You would understand."

The deal was that The School Board would notify him in advance of the date they were releasing the virus and give the exact locations. At that point, he would move all his business interests out of the area, ahead of the disaster that would follow.

He figured it would take the world's governments about a year to come up with the antivirus, produce the vaccine and put a stop to the outbreak—he had already invested in the drug companies he deemed most likely to get that contract. No sense in passing up on an opportunity like that.

He bought canned food and water in immense quantities, for his own needs and for resale once panic erupted. He figured the United Kingdom as a perfect place for storage, not only because he conveniently had a cousin there with a slew of warehouses, but because he figured the British were just too damn polite to loot.

When the time came, he could sell his supplies through an agent and turn a tidy profit.

He planned to spend the year on his private island under complete quarantine and contemplate the power shifts that would occur when five to ten percent of the population of the industrial countries was lost. Obviously, the outbreak wouldn't be as bad in isolated communities in off-the-track areas as it would be in the big cities.

There would be chaos and panic, even a power vacuum in a country or two. And he needed to figure out the best way to make sure that it would be his men who filled them.

WHEN HE SAW the lab's number on the display, Brant picked up his buzzing phone, but kept his attention on the street. "Hey, Chris. What's up?"

"Ballistics are in on the bullet you sent. No match in the database. Looks like we have no previous crime on record that was committed with the same gun."

"Damn," he said without heat. Chris and him went way back. "You think you could call me with some good news just once?"

"Hey, the Stetson case wasn't my fault. Stop hassling me. I should've gone home hours ago. You know what I'm gonna get from the wife when I sneak in in the middle of the night?"

"The rolling pin on the head?"

"Nothing. That's what I'm going to get. No-thing."

"My heart bleeds. It's not the middle of the night, anyway. It's 10:00 p.m."

"I get home after eight, it's the middle of the night to her."

"I guess you better think hard all the way home about how to make it up to her. Need some pointers on how to woo a woman?"

"You're a real joker, you know that?"

"I am known for my excellent sense of humor, as a matter of fact," he said. "Anyway, thanks for the info. Much appreciated."

"Don't mention it."

"And don't tell your wife I'm the reason you're late. I don't want her to drop me from the Christmas list."

"Kiss goodbye to the homemade eggnog," Chris said before he disconnected.

Brant put down the phone and looked up to Anita's window where her silhouette moved back and forth between her dresser and her bed. She was putting away her laundry.

The fingerprint kit he'd asked for had been FedExed to him by midmorning. He'd wasted no time putting it to use. Then, when he was sure he'd gotten all he could, he went through Anita's place with a fine-toothed comb.

She was a neat and orderly woman, and warm, which on the surface of things reminded him a little of his across-the-street neighbor, Eileen, except that, really, they were nothing alike. Anita had exotic foods in her cupboards and dresses in her closet that he was extremely uncomfortable sifting through. Anita's cinnamon-colored eyes danced with life, her generous lips were never too far from a smile. Her body inspired thoughts that were as far as you could get from neighborly.

He didn't want to think about what part that might have played in him being here tonight, protecting her from afar—in addition to the sturdy new dead bolt he'd put on her door. Because this all should have been strictly about the mission. But since Brant Law wasn't the type of man who ran from trouble, he pulled the thing right out into the open and admitted it—at least, to himself.

He had a problem with Anita Caballo.

The way he saw it, he had two choices. Leave the island and order Nick back. Or suck it up, lock up whatever insanity was trying to get a hold of him and stay here.

He had almost kissed her in his hotel room last night, dammit.

That kind of thing couldn't happen. He was the badge. He was held to a certain code of conduct. He held himself to it. He had broken that once, gotten involved with Lynette. The price had been enormous.

Brant looked away from the silhouette that danced on the sheer curtains of her window. He should be back at his hotel in bed. Except the bed she'd spent the night in twice now was giving him trouble, making it hard to rest. You got a woman like that in your bed and the pictures of what could have been were impossible to chase away.

And it wasn't even *his* bed. It was a hotel bed dressed in wild colors, used by God knew how many travelers, impersonal. *His* bed was a four-poster monster at home. He'd made it himself six years ago from hundred-year-old knotty pine when he'd been off duty recovering from a gunshot injury.

He'd signed up for a woodworking class in the evenings at the local high school to keep from going stir-crazy. It turned out to be one of those things where people went just to use the tools, with no more than a passing glance from the instructor. There was no lecture, no homework, no structure of any kind. He'd glanced through the blueprints someone was handing around—printed straight off the Internet—and for some reason the bed spoke to him. Another guy was making a blanket chest for his wife. And old, ornery fellow crafted a coffin. He'd been incensed by the prices and had the mind to save his family the hassle. The old geezer had seemed too stubborn to ever die.

Brant had waited for his leg to heal and made the bed that, in the end, had turned out to be way too big for his bedroom, filling it nearly from wall to wall. He shook his head. Why was he sitting in front of Anita Caballo's apartment at midnight, thinking about her one second and about *his* bed at home, the next?

He should go back to the hotel and get some sleep.

She paused at the window. What was she thinking about? Was she scared?

She hadn't shown it, but she had to be. She'd been attacked twice in the last couple days and the danger wasn't over yet. William hadn't worked alone. Whoever he'd partnered with knew where Anita lived and had been inside her place while she'd been out.

Brant pushed the seat back and stretched his legs as much as was possible. He was getting used to sleeping sitting up. Might as well stay here.

He expected to get word on the fingerprints sometime in the morning. Once he had a name and a face, he could track whoever it was—check credit-card records, figure out hotel, rental-car license plate, whatever—take the guy out. As soon as he was sure that Anita was safe, he would take off, go back home. Nick was coming back anyway.

The women hadn't turned out as he had expected. They'd surprised him. That didn't happen often.

To start with, they had grown into a team that worked pretty well together. And they were committed to the cause. He was beginning to think that they just might stand a chance at getting to Tsernyakov.

He could not compromise the mission by starting anything with Anita. And on a personal level, getting involved with her would be the shortest way to end his career in disgrace.

Think Eileen. Think safe and steady. Think oatmeal cookies. His old comfortable life in his old comfortable neighborhood. Eileen was already part of that picture. That was what he wanted. He was old enough to know what was good for him.

WHY WAS THE MAN watching Anita? Who was he, a bodyguard? But why would she have one? Was she even aware that he was watching?

The woman hiding in her rented van observed the guy in the car, how he took turns between watching the street and Anita's window.

How long would he stay?

The idiot was ruining her plans for the night.

She wanted Anita, wanted answers then wanted to watch her die. She'd waited a long time for this. She had suffered enough because of the bitch. Now it was time to make her pay. Wasn't she going to be surprised?

The woman in the van flashed a self-satisfied grin at the thought. Anita wouldn't suspect her, that's for sure. Wouldn't think she was capable. Anita had always been patronizing, thinking everyone needed her help.

But all they needed was the money and for her to take the fall for it.

And now Anita was out and too smart to let live. It had taken her a while to convince William of that. William who was still nowhere to be found. What had Anita done to him?

To Anita, he was an old boyfriend to be discarded.

To her, William was the love of her life.

She had to get to the bitch to get answers. And Anita would talk, she would make sure of that. And then she would kill her.

She had a plan: shoot her in the knees, making sure she couldn't get away, then work on her for as long as it took to get all the answers she needed, show her who was boss. But first she had to get to her and the man in the car was in her way.

It didn't matter. She was patient. Hadn't she waited years setting up the job? Hadn't she seduced William glance by glance, smile by smile, one word at a time until he was hers?

She was looking forward to seeing the look on Anita's face when she told her that.

"William." She mumbled the word and felt

the fear and pain of not being able to find him. "Where are you?"

The bitch had done something to him. She was unwilling to consider that William would abandon or betray her. He loved her. She was sure of that. William was the real thing, the only man who mattered now in her life. She would find him, save him from Anita if needed. Then he would love her even more.

"I'm coming, my love," she whispered. "I'm coming."

ANITA SAT ON HER BED, picked up her nightgown, then tossed it aside again.

He was outside, guarding her.

Gina would have been ticked that Brant didn't trust her abilities if he'd done the same thing to her. Gina would have gone down to challenge him, to send him away. Probably Carly, too. She had a fierce independent streak. Sam, whom Anita called to make sure she was okay with that nasty cold, would have pretended not to care. Anita was strangely touched by the fact that he would come.

It was unnecessary. She had the gun nearby and she knew how to use it.

But would she?

The thought pushed her to her feet again.

If whoever William had schemed with was someone in her family, what would she do?

Who had been in her apartment? The thought that it could have been someone she knew and loved drove her crazy. Why? The company was theirs, it was for all of them. If someone had financial problems, why not come clean to the others? They were brothers and sisters for heaven's sake.

The possibility of such betrayal hurt more than the last four miserable years in prison.

Questions knocked together in her head like bumper cars, bruising her brain. She wished there was someone she could talk them over with. Then she realized she did have someone, and nearby at that, whose judgment she trusted.

She tucked the handgun into the back of her capri pants and pulled her T-shirt over it then headed out the door. The hallway was deserted, the staircase empty. She waited for the lone car that sped down her street in an obvious hurry to get somewhere, then crossed over to Brant.

He shook his head and hesitated, but popped the lock after a few seconds.

She got in. "Hi."

"You could have called." He was looking straight ahead.

"You could have stayed in your hotel and gotten some rest."

He turned his head and his mahogany gaze locked with hers.

"What are you doing here, Anita?"

The air seemed to heat and thicken in the car all of a sudden. It took effort to fill her lungs.

What were they doing there? She'd come to talk about work, hadn't she?

"I can't sleep. I keep thinking about my family."

"Came up with anything new? Any clues? Even if you don't think it's relevant."

"I just can't get over the shock of it all that any of them could be involved. It seems so unlikely. What if we're wasting time going down the wrong road?"

"What if we're not?"

"It's stupid, but—" she hesitated "—sometimes I feel like I'd almost rather not know."

"Is that why you didn't fight for yourself at your trial?"

Her eyes went wide. "What are you talking about? I fought."

"Not like I would have. You held your lawyer back."

Had she? She hesitated as she thought back.

"I'm not saying you did it on purpose. But maybe your subconscious mind— Maybe you knew there was a good chance that whoever had framed you was close to you and didn't want to find out anything bad about your family."

"My family is *not* bad. You don't know them." She loved them all.

"I know. All I'm saying is that you do need to fight for yourself. Whoever is out there wants to kill you. This game is dead serious. Look, I know it's not easy to face that someone you love, someone you believe in, might have betrayed you. But trust me, if you don't face it, the consequences can be pretty nasty. Not something you want."

He sounded like he was talking from experience.

"Anything like that happen to you?" she asked, partially because she was curious, partially because the thought of someone in her family going against her was too painful.

He didn't respond.

"So who was it?"

He shrugged. "A woman. I thought— Never mind."

"What happened?"

"I didn't take a suspect seriously. She put on the play and I bought it. Brought all my protective instincts right out. My partner died because I was stupid." He looked stiff with regret and self-loathing.

She put a hand on his, not being the type who

could hold back when someone needed comfort or consoling. "I'm sorry."

"So am I. You wouldn't believe how very sorry. So don't make the same mistake. Keep your eyes open. Know who your enemy is."

They sat in silence for a while. One minute passed, then another. When it begin to feel awkward, she pulled her hand away.

"Thank you for everything that you do for me," she said to fill the silence. "I appreciate it. I do feel safer when you're around."

He hesitated before he responded. "It's my job."

The light of the streetlight illuminated his face. He was so handsome and strong and noble it made her heart ache.

He must have read some of her thoughts because he said, "I can't. I'm not going to make the same mistake again."

"I'm not a suspect you're investigating."

The quick flash of heat in his gaze took her breath away. "I'm here to get the job done."

He didn't look like work was the topmost thing on his mind. Fire swirled in his eyes.

"You should go up and get some sleep." His voice was gruff. He turned away, watching the street through the windshield.

That near-moment the night before flashed

into her eyes. "Um. Last night when you— Was that—"

"No." He wouldn't look at her.

"Okay."

"You should probably go back up."

"Right." She didn't move.

He turned to her with a pained expression. "You know you are a very beautiful woman."

Was Brant as attracted to her as she was to him? The thought hit her with the capricious subtlety of a cement truck.

He seemed frustrated by her lack of response. "This is— It's not how this works."

"This what?" She found her voice at last.

"We are on a dangerous mission. We need to focus one-hundred percent on the case and then-some."

"Right." Getting nervous, she licked her bottom lip.

His gaze turned darker. "You're not helping."

He did want her! The thought sang through her veins and sent her heart drumming. She couldn't stop the smile that split her lips.

"Don't look so smug." He turned away from her again.

"I'm not."

"Right."

"So what do you want me to look like, exactly?" she challenged him.

He turned back to her and said something under his breath that she didn't quite catch. Sounded like, "To hell with oatmeal raisin." Obviously, she'd heard it wrong.

And then he leaned right over and kissed her.

The kiss was everything she had expected it to be and more, not that she had spent much time thinking about it. Okay, maybe some. The wave of pure heat and blinding passion and uncompromising need stole the breath from her lungs.

Her brain was rapidly becoming impaired, as well. Her last thought was that she wasn't going to walk away unscathed from this.

THEY WERE KISSING.

She watched from the backseat of her van.

Whore.

It made her sick how Anita worked her poison on the man. Anita Caballo had always known how to make men do what she wanted. She played with them, the same way she had played with William. What had the she done to him now?

It'd been days since he'd checked in and no matter how hard she tried, he could not be reached.

Where was he?

Anita lived.

Which meant William might very well be dead.

And the bitch could sit in that car with her man and do her whoring, rubbing it in her face.

She lifted her gun and aimed, drew a slow breath, held it. A full second passed before she lowered the gun again.

It was too dark, they were too far away, the bullet would have to go through two windshields. She didn't want to take a chance on making a mistake. This was too important. She wasn't just doing this for herself. She was doing this for William.

Chapter Eight

Anita was wading through the numbered accounts Cavanaugh had in Switzerland. How on earth had Carly gotten to these? The kid was a genius. She glanced up at the sound of the office door opening and felt a pang of disappointment when, instead of Brant, she saw Nick walking in.

He was tall and muscular, looking like the commando guy that he was—cute and sexy, to boot. He didn't interest her whatsoever. *Diosmio,* she had it bad for Brant.

"Missed me?" He grinned as he looked around.

Gina was coming out of her office. "Like we miss lockdown."

"Aww." Nick put a hand to his heart and flashed a heat wave of a grin. "You make me feel all soft and fuzzy."

"There are pills that can help with that now,"

Gina said dryly, but she had a half-smile on her face.

Anita sent the screen she was working with to the printer then got up and walked out of her office. "Hi."

"What's up?" Sam was asking as Nick dropped his duffel bag by the front desk. She still sounded nasal, but looked a lot better.

Carly was coming out of her den, too. "How was your trip? Good to have you back."

He smiled at her. "It's good to be back. Coffee?" He started toward the kitchen.

"Probably sludge at this stage. I'll make a fresh pot," Sam volunteered.

Five people in the small kitchenette filled it to the brim, but nobody seemed to mind.

"Brant sleeping on the job, or what?" He went for a mug.

Hopefully Brant *was* sleeping, Anita thought. He needed the rest after having spent the whole night in front of her apartment, guarding her. He drove her to work in the morning and walked her up before he left. Their conversation had been limited to polite conversation about traffic and the weather. "He was here earlier. He's working out of his hotel room."

The coffee machine began to spit its black brew, filling the air with a mouthwatering aroma.

"So what do you have on Xiau Lin?" Gina asked.

"My bet is he's not linked to Tsernyakov. I'd say they're rivals to a degree. I found some conflicting operations. Tsernyakov would never allow that."

"So he's off the list?" Carly asked.

Nick nodded. "I checked into Alexeev, too, on the way back. He was definitely heavily involved with Tsernyakov on the island—probably Tsernyakov's number-one guy—but I found out that he's gone for good. Disappeared."

"Dead gone?" Carly put sugar and milk on the table. "It takes forty-two coffee beans to make an espresso."

Nobody batted an eyelash. They were used to her habit of spouting old trivia.

"Either that or he was abducted by aliens. Nobody knows anything about him. Somebody took over the majority of his businesses, can't get an ID on the new guy, but orders are coming down the food chain. And get this, Alexeev's on-the-side money, blackmail and bribes and whatnot—good chunks of cash Tsernyakov probably didn't know about—they're still coming in, piling up. His old assistant is hoarding it all. Doesn't dare to report it to the new guy, in case Alexeev shows up. But if he doesn't show up and the secret stash comes to light, the new boss will pop him for it. Guy's a mess."

Coffee was done. Nick picked up the pot and poured for everyone.

"So we need to figure out who the new man in charge is," Carly said.

"Right. And I'll need your help with that." He picked up his cup. "I have a couple of ideas on where to look."

After the two of them had gone off to Carly's office, Anita found herself lingering in the kitchenette with Gina and Sam. "It's not good, is it?"

Gina shook her head. "We had a handful of tenuous leads. Emphasis on tenuous. We are down to two: Cavanaugh and Marquez."

"They're both dirty." Anita had plenty of financial records to prove that.

"But are they connected to Tsernyakov?"

Gina was right. That was the crux of the matter.

"They are some of the biggest players on the island. We know Tsernyakov has connections here. A man as big as he is wouldn't be doing business with small-timers," Sam said.

Gina was watching Carly and Nick working in Carly's office. She had an amused expression on her face, so Anita followed her gaze.

"So what? You think they're doing it?" Sam caught on.

What? Anita looked closer. Okay, so maybe Nick was standing a little too close, bending a little too low.

"Like rabbits." Gina grinned and shook her head.

"None of our business." Anita came to Carly's defense. She was certainly not one to cast a stone. Not after fogging up the windshield with Brant last night. God, she was so not going to think about that right now.

Gina nodded. "More power to them."

"How is your fiancé?" Sam teased her.

"We spend time together. Lots of good quiet times. He's the strong silent type," Gina said.

"Always lets you have the last word?" Anita grinned.

"Damn right."

Gina's "fiancé" was pinned to the wall by her computer—a job done by Sam, after Gina said she believed in love at first sight and pointed to the cover of a Chinese business magazine and said of the man who looked like an English aristocrat, "That's the man I'm going to marry."

"Know who he is yet?" Sam asked.

"Haven't had a chance to brush up on my Chinese." Gina shrugged.

"Not knowing the groom's name must put an inconvenient hold on ordering the wedding invitations," Anita put in.

"Oh, hell, no." Gina snorted. "Can you see me prancing around in a hooped gown?"

Anita squinted. No. She couldn't.

"We're eloping."

"Glad to hear the plans are all set," Sam said stone-faced. "Little disappointed about not being a bridesmaid. Understandable, though. Bride not wanting to be outshined on her big day. Carly and I *were* runners-up to Beach Beauty and all that."

"Bite me," Gina said, picked up her mug and walked out of the kitchen.

They followed her after a moment.

"Good morning, ladies." The mailman was coming in. Garry, a young blond guy, was cute as a button, swishing his behind with more panache than Angelina Jolie.

"Morning. Got anything good?" Sam walked toward him and took the handful of flyers and letters.

"Yeah, but they don't let me share it with postal customers," he told her with a wink. "Regulations are a bitch."

"Live dangerously."

He gave an overexaggerated shiver. "I used to, sweetling. Residential delivery. Ugh. You should have seen the nasty dogs. Nice businessmen in mmm, mmm suits. Now, that's better." His eyes caught Nick in Carly's office and went wide. "Or cargo pants. Works for me," he said.

"I don't think he swings that way." Sam followed his gaze.

He sighed. "Life is a friggin' heartbreak a day. Still, we must look on the bright side. New lawyer's office coming in on floor ten. Major big thing. All men."

"Good luck," Sam said.

He cast one last glance at Nick before leaving.

"Anything for me?" Anita asked, shaking her head, but smiling.

Sam was flipping through the envelopes. "The usual. Bills and junk mail. No. Wait. This looks promising." She held out a fancy envelope with a gold-foil logo in the top left corner— Lambert Estates.

Anita opened it and pulled out an engraved invitation in mauve. "They're having an impromptu party Saturday night to celebrate their five-hundredth client. The Cayman Paradise Hotel Resort signed them on for a total rebuild. The party will be on the hotel's private beach and will end with a charity event to benefit dolphin rescue."

"What kind of charity event?" Sam asked.

"Maybe you'll luck out and it'll be a bachelor auction," Gina told her.

"Maybe we'll luck out and it'll be an annoying-ex-cop auction. Do you think they'd accept another one this close to the date?" Sam retorted.

Anita turned the paper over and played along. "The invite doesn't say."

Gina ignored them, looking thoughtful. "Probably everyone who's anyone will be there. We should be able to make some good connections. Maybe one of our remaining suspects will show and we get a chance to cozy up to him."

Right. They had to figure which one was Tsernyakov's connection on the island.

Sam pointed to the last gold-lettered line. "They're promising an explosive ending."

"Oh, I like fireworks," Anita said.

SHE COULD SEE THEM TALK. She had picked the hotel for that specific purpose, so that she could keep an eye on Anita during the day. If she was like she'd been before, she would spend most of her time at work.

Searching Anita's apartment had netted no clues on the whereabouts of William. She was beginning to fear the worst.

She wanted answers and she wanted satisfaction. And, most of all, she wanted to make sure that her secret died with the bitch.

ANITA SET THE PHONE DOWN with a grin.

"Good news?" Brant stood in her doorway.

"Marquez is coming over this afternoon. We had an appointment for next week. I was supposed to go to him, but he just called me to let me know that he'll be in the neighborhood for a business meeting this afternoon and if I can bring up our meeting he'd be glad to stop in."

"Excellent."

"Except that we lose the chance to plant some bugs in his office."

"But we gain the fact that we can all check him out, get some impressions. I'll be here as another prospective client, talking with Gina."

"Do you want to meet him?"

He hesitated. "No," he said after a while. "I don't want to risk personal contact. It's your mission. I just want to take the measure of the man."

"Cavanaugh is coming back tonight." Carly popped her head in the office. "Flight plan was just filed."

"Then he might be coming to the party Saturday." Relief filled Anita.

"Pretty good chance," Brant said. "Seems like the type of guy who likes to be seen around. There'll be media for the charity angle."

"If he is there, we'll make contact," Gina said.

"I'm going to take off for a while, check into a couple things. Everyone's okay here?" he asked.

"Young as we seem, we really don't need a babysitter," Gina quipped.

Brant drew up an eyebrow. "Didn't mean to imply that you do. Call me if you need me."

And it hit Anita as he walked away that she did need him—in so many ways that it was getting to be scary. It wasn't an easy admission to make.

"To be honest, Señorita Caballo, my main priority is to scale back. So I am looking for help with that instead of establishing an office. I already have offices and employees, but it's becoming all too big. I'm downsizing."

"May I ask why you are cutting back, Señor Marquez?"

"I'm thinking about retirement."

"You're way too young to retire."

He smiled. "That might be true, but my even younger wife is going to gift me with twin boys a few months from now. I have decided to spend more time with them than I did with the children from my first marriage." He took a long breath. "The business has been good to me, I've been lucky not to— I've been lucky." He smiled again.

Lucky he hadn't gotten caught, Anita finished the sentence for him silently. She was familiar with his financial records, courtesy of Carly. There were enough illegitimate sources of income to put a smile on any D.A.'s face.

"I understand," she said. "Family first."

"Exactly. I don't have to worry about money. My children won't have to worry about it, either. I want to take a break and live a little."

"How can we help you?"

"I will need outplacement services for a good fifty percent of my employees. I need to sell off unnecessary equipment. I would like the company to move into a smaller office or to divide the existing one and rent out the unused portion."

"We can certainly do that."

"I will also need some data to be removed from our equipment for encryption and storage."

"No problem." Was he going legit in anticipation of the birth of his sons? Or was he scaling back his existing business because he'd gotten some better paying projects from Tsernyakov? "Will you be doing a lot of global business in the future? Are you keeping your overseas interests? Our IT specialist has a number of innovative techniques that you might want to employ in that area."

"I'll be selling my global interests," he said. "With the new family, I am hoping to spend a lot more time at home."

She nodded and mentally crossed him off the list. Sounded like he was taking several large steps back from business life. The man Tsernyakov chose to replace Alexeev would be moving in the opposite direction. Looked like they were down to a single suspect: Cavanaugh.

But what if they succeeded in getting close to him and ended up realizing he was just a solitary crook, with no connections whatsoever to Tsernyakov? Would they have to start everything all over again? She wondered if Brant already had plans in place for that. He would. He was organized and systematic—virtues that fit well with her accountant-type personality.

Anita focused on Marquez. She was *not* going to sit here and think about how well Brant and she fitted together in a number of ways. She needed to get real and get the man out of her head.

Anita glanced at the corner of her screen. It was seven-thirty in the evening already; nobody but her and Carly were in the office.

"Hook him and reel him in," Carly said, and headed for the kitchen, probably for more coffee. She often worked late, got caught up in whatever program she was running.

Anita looked at the information on her laptop. What was she still doing here? She could have looked at these figures at her apartment, settled into her couch. But she'd been waiting for Brant and Brant hadn't come.

She'd gotten used to him watching over her. How stupid was that? She'd agreed to a dangerous mission. She couldn't expect him to hold her hand the whole way.

She turned off the laptop and tossed it in its case then stood. "I'm going home," she called out to Carly who was still in the kitchen.

"Brant's here?" She stuck her head out.

"I think I can handle it on my own."

"Maybe he's working on something with Nick. Debriefing each other or whatever. You should wait." She disappeared, but a second later popped out again. "Want me to take you home?"

"I'll be fine." Did Brant go back to the States without saying anything? It was possible. He could have left just as he had arrived—without notice. The thought hit her hard in the chest. He'd come to keep on eye on them while Nick had been away. Now that Nick was back, he probably figured he wasn't necessary.

"Never mind. I'm gonna go, anyway." Carly shut off the kitchen light behind her. "Which car do you want to take?"

"I don't have mine. Brant brought me in."

"You were going to walk?" Carly stopped for

a second and just stared at her. "You shouldn't take any chances."

"You're right."

They turned off the lights and locked up, took the elevator down to the lobby.

"So what's up with Nick?" Anita asked.

Carly shrugged, but wouldn't look at her. "He's back."

"Carly Jones." Anita smiled. "I meant, beyond that?"

"He is okay."

Obviously, Carly didn't want to talk about it. She was okay with that. Everyone was entitled to their privacy.

"Yes, he is," Anita said. "All I meant was that if you're happy, I'm happy for you."

They reached the lobby level and said good-night to the security guard at the desk, stepped out into the muggy night. The wave of heat that hit them in the face came as a shock after the building's air-conditioned climate.

The first thing she saw was Brant's car and him behind the wheel, talking on his cell phone. Relief flooded her and a smile that she couldn't hold back split her face. She looked at Carly to tell her that she'd be going home with Brant and found her watching.

"So what's up with Brant?" Carly asked, a smile playing above her lips.

"He'll take me home. Thanks for the offer, anyway."

"Beyond that."

She tried to look as nonchalant as she could. "He's a nice guy."

Carly pulled up an eyebrow. "Spill."

"Hey, I let the Nick business go."

"So? Who said life was fair?"

"There's nothing to tell."

"I bet not for long." Carly flashed an all-knowing grin. "Try to have a fun night." She made smooching moves as she walked away.

Oh, for heaven's sake, what were they, teenagers? Anita thought, but couldn't help smiling.

Brant leaned over and pushed the passenger side door open for her, still on the phone. She got in.

"Okay. Thanks." He hung up. "Sorry. I got bogged down on the phone. I was going to come up. Any news?"

"I think we can cross Marquez off the list, for now." She told him about her meeting with the man and the conclusions she had drawn.

He seemed to agree with her.

"How about you? Find out anything new?"

The look on his face said it wasn't going to be anything she liked.

"Got the results on the fingerprints. One clear set other than Carly's, Gina's, Sam's, Nick's, yours and mine. No match in any of the databases."

Disappointment balled in her stomach. She'd placed so much hope in those prints. "So that's a dead end."

He pulled away from the curb and into traffic. "Don't worry about it. We'll catch whoever it is. How is work?"

"Okay." She had to spend most of her day on the legit business, since that was picking up. "Cavanaugh is coming back tonight." She'd almost forgotten. "And we're invited to a beach party this weekend."

"Whose?"

"Michael Lambert."

He pulled up an eyebrow, but didn't say anything.

"It's not like that."

"It's none of my business."

She hated the bitter taste of disappointment that rose in her throat. "So whatever it takes, one of us is going to make personal contact with Cavanaugh if he's there. We are going to try to entice him into some business, legit or otherwise."

They discussed that for the few minutes it took to get to her building. He got out to walk her up.

"You'll stay down here again tonight?"

He nodded.

"It's not necessary."

"Just the same."

She didn't want him to stay. It was too hard to try to sleep knowing he was just outside her bedroom window. But, of course, she couldn't tell him that.

"Don't you have anything else to do?"

"Nothing that won't keep."

And from the way he said that, she felt like he did have something in mind to investigate. "So what am I keeping you from?"

He paused so long she didn't think he would respond, but then he said, "I thought about swinging by and checking out Cavanaugh's place from the oceanside. Didn't see much the other night. Figure that end would be wide-open."

"You just want to get on the water." She remembered his earlier comment on loving boats.

"That, too." He grinned.

She considered for a moment. Her choices were tossing sleeplessly in bed, or doing something that might move the mission forward.

"Give me a second to change into something more suitable for spying on the high seas," she said.

THEY SHOULD HAVE gotten separate WaveRunners. Brant cut the motor, breathed easier once Anita's arms slid from around his waist. Bringing her was the best option for the mission—this way, he could make sure she was safe and do some surveillance at Cavanaugh's place at the same time—but he wasn't sure it was the best thing for him.

The moon glinted off the water with enough romantic flair for a postcard, the air balmy, the water only a few degrees colder. The Cavanaugh estate was about a thousand feet down the beach. He had to start thinking about that instead of what Anita's breasts had felt like pressed against his back as they had ridden the waves.

"These come in handy." Anita was gesturing at the sleek vehicle that brought them so far.

"Best invention since the motorboat," he said. "I'm going in." He pulled his T-shirt over his head, draped it over the handlebars and slid into the water. He needed a little cooling off.

He let the WaveRunner slowly drift with the waves and floated along with it.

Twenty minutes passed before they were in line with the Cavanaugh estate. They had an unobstructed view of the mansion itself from here. The main building was dark, but another, maybe a guest cottage, on the other side of the driveway had light filtering through drawn blinds.

"I'll snap some pictures," Anita said.

She was using his camera, not her ring gadget.

This one had serious zooming power and could operate under less-than-ideal light conditions.

"Make sure you get the neighboring estates, too." He paddled in place.

A light came on at the end of Cavanaugh's private marina, then blinked out again. Nothing but a speedboat was docked there tonight, although Cavanaugh had several watercrafts registered under his name.

The waves were pushing the WaveRunner toward the shore, so he grabbed on to it and swam to keep it at a safe distance where they wouldn't be seen, or if they were, their presence wouldn't cause alarm. A man and a woman out on the water on a moonlit night like this was a pretty common occurrence in a tourist paradise. They were floating along the waves about three hundred feet from the beach, passing the estate's boundary now. The light at the end of the marina blinked on again, then went out.

"Looks like the salt air's gotten to the wiring," Anita said.

"Maybe. My guess would be that it's a signal."

"For whom?"

"We'll have to stick around to see."

They floated by the next property. The pink mansion had a couple lights on upstairs and cars in the driveway. Same with the Mediterranean-style villa that came after that. The next property was smaller with a regular house, similar to his aunt's cottage on Rhode Island where he used to spend his summers with his cousins when they'd been kids. This place seemed deserted. He moved to the other side of the WaveRunner and helped the waves push it to shore.

"What if someone sees us?" Anita asked.

"They'll think we're a couple of lovers, sneaking ashore to make love in the surf."

He could see in the moonlight as her breath hitched, and cursed himself for saying that. He didn't need to put that picture into his own head, either. He swam in silence and tried to focus on that, put his back into it, needing to burn off some of the excess energy that vibrated through his body.

She hopped into the cresting waves once they were close enough and helped to pull the Wave-Runner onto shore.

"I'll go up to the house and make sure there's no one here," he said, and moved in the direction of the building, which stood on stilts a good eight feet off the ground. The owner kept a picnic table there with chairs. Not a bad idea—a comfortable spot, always in the shade.

He rounded the structure and made his way to the front where wooden steps led up to the wraparound porch. A sign with the words For Sale and a phone number printed on it blocked half of the downstairs window to the right of the front door. He walked up the steps with caution just the same and peeked in another window. Enough moonlight filtered in from the back to see that the room he was looking at, the living room most likely, was bare, without a single piece of furniture. He checked the rest of the windows and found the same everywhere.

He walked back to Anita and dropped to the sand next to her. She was panning the ocean with the military-issue binoculars he had brought.

"Find anything?" she asked.

"Nobody here. How about you?"

"There is a good-sized boat coming in." She handed the binoculars over to him.

The light at the Cavanaugh estate blinked on again.

He watched the boat that came from the south, parallel to the beach. It was a brand-new, twenty-eight-foot Monticello that seemed to be slowing.

"Movement on the shore," Anita warned.

He shifted his binoculars to Cavanaugh's private beach. The dark van that had been sitting in the driveway was going down the sand now, to the edge of the water. When it got there, a half-dozen men got out. Two of them waded into the water then swam out to the speedboat. A moment later, the boat's motor started up.

"They're going out to the ship," Anita said.

"They're probably too far, but try to take some pictures anyway." He kept his eyes glued to the binoculars.

The ship slowed and the speedboat sidled up to it. There was movement on board on both vessels. Small packages, a foot by a foot maybe, were tossed from the ship to the boat. He counted forty-six of them. Drugs, not illegal immigrants, were the game tonight.

The speedboat brought its cargo back to the van where the packages changed hands once more. The ship continued on toward the main harbor. It probably had a legitimate itinerary, doing a little dirty business on the side.

He got up to go for the WaveRunner at the same time as Anita was rising. They bumped into each other. He lifted a hand to her shoulder to steady her and found that he didn't want to let go. Her gaze shot up to meet his. She didn't pull away as he trailed his fingers down her arm.

It seemed like the most natural thing in the world to wrap his fingers around her wrist and pull her closer.

He should let her go, walk up the beach to his car, drive straight to the airport and get out of here, leave the rest to the women and Nick. The thought ambled through his head. He kissed her instead.

It left him with a craving that clouded his mind to a dangerous degree. The second kiss brought him down—as clean a shot as he'd ever seen. He was old enough to know that he wasn't going to be able to run from this even if he moved to Alaska first thing in the morning. Part of him would be here on this beach, in the moonlight with the waves cresting at his feet, holding Anita in his arms, and the rest of him would have to return or he would never be whole again. He wanted the heat, the spice, the sheer joyful zest of life Anita brought to him.

She made his blood drum with desire and he kissed her deeply and hungrily, hands shooting out to claim. She did the same, giving as good as she got, taking him as he took her, laughing as they tumbled into the surf.

He felt ten years younger. Hell, twenty. Had he ever experienced this overwhelming urgency even back then? If he had, he didn't remember it.

He cupped his palms over her breasts, over the wet tank top that clung to them. They rolled until he was on the bottom and she sprawled on top, her hair cascading around them. "You look like a mermaid in the moonlight."

She rose up and straddled him. "We are going to have sand in some uncomfortable places."

"I feel no pain," he said.

She smiled and traced his face with a finger. He caught it between his teeth when she got to his mouth.

"You look like a shark in the moonlight." She grinned.

"Funny that you should mention that. I do feel predatory." He rose and flipped them, pinning her on the bottom. Then he pulled back, giving her room, a last chance to get away. "Swim for your life."

She ran her fingers up his sides. "Mermaids don't retreat."

"What do they do?"

"This." She pressed her lips to his.

His body told him this was right, this was what he needed, what they both needed. His brain, however, was transmitting the same signal over and over again: *Wrong course of mission. Abort immediately. Abort.*

Chapter Nine

She'd never imagined it could be like this again. She'd never come close with any other man since Miguel. But here in the surf under the moonlit sky, Brant made her forget about the past. She floated on the sheer pleasure of his touch.

A bigger wave washed over them without warning and they came up laughing and gasping for air. He sat up and pulled her into his arms, brushed his lips over hers again, smiling. Then something switched and the next minute he was staring at her with something akin to shock flashing across his face. He looked away and stood abruptly.

"I'm sorry. This is— We can't do this."

She looked up at him, bewildered, speechless for a long moment before she could force, "It's okay," past the sudden lump in her throat.

He extended a hand to her, pulled her to standing. "We should go." The look in his eyes was raw, his body hard with suppressed passion.

The sudden switch of emotions was giving her whiplash. She stared at him, trying to figure out what was going on in his head.

"We have to be smarter than this. I didn't mean to— It was my fault."

She wasn't ready to call what had happened between them a mistake just yet. "You didn't take advantage of me," she said for the record, in case that was what he was worrying about. Although, to a degree, she supposed she understood him. From his point of view, he was here to protect the women on the team, to supervise them. And he was professional enough and gallant enough to consider any other type of conduct unacceptable.

She opened her mouth to make some kind of an argument, to open some dialogue between them on the subject, but he was dragging the WaveRunner into the water already.

"We should get the pictures to Carly, see what she can make of them," he said.

"THIS WILL TAKE a while," Carly said as she hit the Enter key. "There are millions of mug shots in the CIA and FBI databases. Slow work."

Brant watched how Nick—who had the apartment next to Carly's and had come over when

Brant and Anita had arrived—stood by her chair, the comfortable aura around them. Something was going on there.

"Now, let's take a look at this ship." Carly brought the digital picture Anita had taken from the beach onto the screen.

She could barely make out the cabin windows. The image was too dark and too fuzzy, the ship had been too far.

A window of controls appeared at the bottom of the screen as Carly worked. She was adjusting contrast and colors. A couple minutes into it, they were getting somewhere.

"Let's try to look at the negative," she said, and adjusted something else.

They could see where the name of the ship was, a blurry strip of white on the black background.

"Can you zoom in a little more?" Brant asked.

She shook her head. "That only works in the movies. You can't increase resolution. The picture is whatever resolution you took it as. I can enlarge, play with colors and contrast and all that, but that's it."

"So it's a dead end?" Anita was asking.

"Not yet. I'm going to run it through this character recognition program I've been playing around with."

Brant stepped closer. "How does that work?"

"Basically, the computer guesses what letters the shadows look most like," Nick was saying, and Carly nodded.

Carly ran her fingers over the keyboard and more windows appeared. In one of them the fuzzy image of the name began to reshuffle, pixel by pixel. The four of them stood there, eyes glued to the screen. Long seconds ticked by. Nobody said a word. Then finally the blob was beginning to take shape, distinct lines emerging here and there.

AYTRAR II

"Can that be right?" Anita looked up from the screen, her gaze meeting Brant's.

"I can check if a ship by that name is in the international registry." Carly was already accessing the database. "This might take a few minutes."

"Coffee, anyone?" Nick headed to the kitchen and pulled mugs from the cabinets. He sure looked like he felt at home at Carly's place.

"None for me," Brant said. He hoped to catch some sleep after they were done here.

"I'll take a cup." Carly played the keyboard like a piano virtuoso.

"Me, too," Anita said.

He walked out of the kitchen and sat on the couch in the living room, set his mind to Carly and Nick because he didn't want to think about

Anita and himself. Had those two crossed the line? Did he have a right to judge, considering he had come so maddeningly close to doing something on that beach that both Anita and he would have regretted?

One second he was all clear and certain of his future. Eileen, two kids, a boy and a girl, she would still teach. He could see those kids in their school uniforms getting off the bus at the end of his driveway. The next second he was drunk with the sight and feel and taste of Anita and couldn't think beyond the very second, beyond having her. It was madness, brought on by the heat and the fact that she was unlike the women he was normally around.

At work, his female colleagues were competent and professional. If they looked sexy, he didn't notice it because he wasn't supposed to and he was always swamped with work up to his ears. In his private life there had been Eileen, although they hadn't yet passed beyond friendship. The rest of the women on his street were married and he didn't socialize beyond neighbors, colleagues and family. He hadn't had the time or the energy to put himself out there.

The effect Anita Caballo had on him came as a surprise. A surprise he wasn't going to ponder any further. He took a slow breath and focused back on

Nick and Carly, caught an easy glance and a half-smile that passed between them. Oh, hell. Something was going on there, all right. They would have to have a talk. He wasn't looking forward to that. He had a feeling Nick Tarasov could be damn hardheaded when he thought the occasion called for it.

"Bingo!" Carly shot out of her chair and was grinning from ear to ear.

"What is it?" Anita moved closer.

Brant stood.

"The AYTRAR II is under Kazakh flag, registered to a company that's owned by another company that's owned by Peter Alexeev."

Excitement was a palpable thing in the room. This was the biggest breakthrough in the case so far. They had finally identified the link to Tsernyakov—Philippe Cavanaugh.

ANITA SCANNED THE BEACH and made visual contact with Sam, Carly and Gina. They were easy to pick out. All four of them had dressed to be noticed. Nick and Brant, on the other hand, were here without an invite and as such, were blending in someplace. She couldn't spot either, although she had scanned the sand from the edge of the water to the cement barricades on the other side of the hotel.

"Splendid costume," the woman next to her said, dressed as a pirate's parrot, stunning feather headpiece included. It had to be extremely hot. The day had been a scorcher, which even the evening breeze coming off the ocean hadn't tempered yet.

"Thank you." Anita smiled politely. She was dressed as a Caribbean princess in a colorful ruffled skirt with a corset top—it held her small gun without being noticeable. "I love your outfit, too. Very imaginative."

The woman flashed her a gracious smile before disappearing into the crowd.

Anita swayed to the beat of the steel drums. The music was contagious—she couldn't keep still if she wanted to. The dance was in her blood.

Motors roared a hundred feet or so down the beach where a four-wheeler obstacle course had been set up for the pleasure of the guests who thought dancing was too tame an entertainment.

"I'm glad you came."

The familiar voice made her turn. Michael Lambert stood behind her in the flowing robes of an Arabian prince, his gaze caressing her dress with approval.

"Thanks for the invite."

"My pleasure." He reached out a hand. "Would you dance with me?"

She was supposed to keep an eye out for Cavanaugh, but she could do that while dancing. No sense in offending their host. She let him lead her out to the middle of the dance floor.

The man could move, she realized after the first few seconds and gave herself over to the joy of dancing. After a while, she became aware of the sensation that somebody was watching her. She glanced at the circle of guests in various costumes who ringed the dance floor. Many of them had masks on. She took a better look at the men as Michael twirled her. Brant and Nick came separately from the women. She had no idea what costumes they wore.

The song ended and the band switched to a slower number. Michael pulled her in close and touched his lips to her cheek. She looked up, surprised, and pulled back, just as Brant's tight voice came from behind her.

"May I cut in?"

"Certainly." Michael nodded with a rueful smile. "It was a pleasure. I'll see you later."

She couldn't form a response. All she could do was stare at Brant in his pirate-of-the-high-seas outfit.

"Pirate boots?" She got the words out finally.

"Mock me and die, matey."

She grinned. "Am I supposed to say something like, shiver me timbers?"

"Yes, sir, Captain, your request is my command, would be enough."

She grinned. "You might want to pick a hobby to keep you busy. It'll be a long wait."

Oddly the whole getup seemed to fit the man. He hadn't shaved and his five-o'clock shadow gave him a swarthy, dangerous look. The sword in his belt looked all too real. He had on black pants and a worn gray eighteenth-century army coat, a wide belt with a big brass buckle. He was nothing like the pirate-dressed models on the covers of romance novels. He looked dangerous enough to pass for the real thing. His dark eyes were hard, throwing off lightning.

"What is the nature of your interest in Michael Lambert?" he asked as he pulled her close.

She felt a moment of thrill and fear, then realized they were supposed to be dancing. She swayed with him to the music.

"None beyond being polite to the man. We danced."

"I saw that." His words had an edge to them as sharp as his sword. All humor was gone from his face now.

They were body-to-body and she got lost in the storm of his gaze as they moved together.

Dancing with Brant was nothing like dancing with Michael. There was no comparison between the two men. Michael might have been smoother, but Brant possessed an elemental force that knocked the air from her lungs and made the surrounding world disappear. Dancing with Michael, she had no trouble scanning the crowd for Cavanaugh. In Brant's arms, she wouldn't have noticed if Carlos Santana had arrived in a golden chariot.

She liked his inherent strength, his focus, his unyielding integrity. And she liked the way her body woke up around him. He made her feel things she hadn't thought she would feel again, was scared and excited about. And as she relaxed in his arms, she realized that Brant Law was a man she could fall in love with.

That snapped her to attention.

Diosmio, was she ready for that?

Was he?

The time and the place was all wrong, for sure. She was involved in a mission that was more dangerous than anything she had ever done in her life. And yet she felt the tug, the slip of control, emotions taking over. That brought a swift flash of panic and she pulled away.

What was she thinking? They had some mutual attraction going, something that she wouldn't have minded discovering under normal circumstances. She drew the line at love. Not now and definitely not with this man. They didn't fit into each other's lives.

"Do you mind if we stop? It's too hot. I need a little walk." She was already stepping away.

"I'll come with you."

"No." She needed to escape and round up her common sense, scare it out from wherever it was hiding. "Thanks. I'm just going down to the beach."

She kicked off her sandals at the edge of the dancing platform and nearly ran to the water, didn't stop until the balmy waves lapped at her ankles. She wasn't falling in love, she told herself. She was just dazzled by the man. And why not? He was pretty impressive. A perfectly normal reaction on her part. She couldn't be falling for him. Look at the occupation he was in. She wouldn't have a peaceful moment in her life.

A couple sat on the sand kissing twenty feet or so to her left, so she walked to the right. Far ahead, a group of people were splashing each other. She recognized two as clients of Savall.

Her top dug into her skin. "I hate corsets," she muttered.

"Did you know women stopped wearing those to be patriotic?" Carly said through her earpiece. "In 1917. It freed up 28,000 tons of metal for the war effort."

"Should that make me feel better?" Anita groused, but couldn't help but smile. She was always amazed at the amount of information in Carly's head.

She walked on and reached the group at the water's edge at the same time as Michael Lambert did, coming from the other direction.

"Enjoying the party?"

She forced a smile on her face. "It's great. I have a feeling people won't forget this one anytime soon."

"Buy any raffle tickets?"

"About a dozen." Even though they were a hundred dollars each. But the kind of people who'd been invited were expected to be able to afford them. "I believe in dolphin rescue."

"Yet another thing we have in common." He ran a finger down her arm.

She didn't pull away this time. She wanted to keep him around long enough to ask some questions. "Nice turnout. Any local celebrities here I should know?"

"Mostly business people."

"All very important, I assume," she prompted him.

He laughed. "They like to think so. I think the demolition gimmick worked. Almost everyone who was invited showed. We'll draw the winning raffle ticket at midnight and the winner gets to push the red button to bring the building down. The waterfront gets a new resort and the dolphin rescue gets a nice shot in the arm."

"And your company gets a healthy contract?" she asked.

He grinned at her. "See? Isn't it perfect? Everybody will be happy."

"Must have taken you forever to set this up."

He shrugged. "The demolition, yes. The party was a last-minute addition. The client insisted on it. They wanted the publicity it's going to bring. Safety is a nightmare, though. We removed every single window to prevent broken glass from flying and took out as much metal as we could. Can't risk it turning into shrapnel during the explosions. You have no idea what just the insurance for the party cost—" He stopped himself and gave her an apologetic smile. "But enough about business. Have you been to the treasure hunt yet?" He pointed toward the dozens of small white buoys that bobbed on the water. "There's a treasure chest at the end of each line. Would you like to have a go?"

Now that she looked closer, she could see the heads on the water, too. There were people who had already swum out there, at least a dozen. If

Cavanaugh was one of them, with Michael by her side, she could gain a quick introduction.

"Sure."

He was taking off his clothes already and she joined him. Everyone had their bathing suits on under their costumes, as specified on the invitation. Her mike was hidden in a flower pinned to her top, her gun secured under her corset. With her back to Michael, she wrapped the gun into the bandana that had been tied around her arm and buried it a few inches under the sand, then tossed her clothes over it. Even if someone accidentally stepped on her clothes, which shouldn't happen—tiki torches stuck in the sand provided plenty of light to see—the metal ribs of the corset would disguise the shape of the weapon. In any case, she didn't have the option of a better hiding place. And she sure couldn't take it into the water. She would be gone only a few minutes. She took her earpiece out, as well, not sure if the transmitter would survive the ocean, pretending she was taking off her large hoop clip-ons.

The water enveloped her body like a comforting caress, the gentle waves providing just enough challenge to take her mind off Brant. It felt good to cool off, to stretch her body and get her muscles moving. She used to love swimming. And it seemed she still could put some power into it. Michael and she reached the line of buoys at about the same time.

"Good luck. Grab whatever looks good to you." He winked at her before he submerged.

She held on to the line and felt her way down, found a crate of bottles maybe ten feet from the surface, identifying them by feel. Not enough moonlight filtered down to see more than shadows. She grabbed a bottle then let go of the line and kicked away, rising to the surface.

"Champagne," she said when Michael came up next to her. "What did you get?"

He held up a large key that looked like a theater prop. "A free night at the hotel when it opens." He passed it to her. "For you. Since I'm the developer, I get to wrangle free nights anyway."

"Thanks."

"Michael," somebody was shouting from the shore. "Is that you out there?"

"Go away, Philippe. I'm busy."

Philippe? The air caught in Anita's lungs as she focused on the man who stood on the shore, a woman on each arm. Was that Philippe Cavanaugh? The height and body type seemed right.

"It's okay. I need to go out there anyway. The champagne is heavy," she said.

"I can hold it for you if you want to go down

to look for more treasure." Mike reached out a hand.

She paddled water. "We can always come back in."

"Okay."

Cavanaugh was walking off.

"Race you," Anita said, and threw herself into swimming.

They made it to shore head-to-head. Which didn't prevent Michael from claiming victory.

"And now my prize," he said, as he reached out with his free hand and pulled her to him, brushed his lips against hers.

It didn't feel unpleasant, but there was no compulsion to linger, no wave of need and passion as it had been with Brant. She pulled away.

He watched her for a long moment, his expression thoughtful. "It's not there, is it?"

She shook her head.

"Stuff with the big guy, it's the real thing?" he asked with a rueful smile.

"I think so." That was a scary admission to make.

He nodded. "If it doesn't turn out to be, you know where to find me. I better go see if the big finale is all set up." He gave her another smile before he turned and walked away.

Cavanaugh and the women had stopped a few

feet from the water's edge. Anita walked that way, as if she were on her way back to the dancing. She needed an excuse to talk to them.

It hadn't been necessary. Cavanaugh recognized her.

"Hello. Anita, right? Nice work at the Beach Beauty Pageant."

"Thanks." She gave him her best smile and ignored the glares from the other women.

"Friend of Michael?"

"Business acquaintance." It wasn't strictly true, but they did meet at a business function and she wanted to bring business into the conversation.

Cavanaugh put his hands to the small of the women's back and pushed them forward gently. "Why don't you girls go and see what treasures you can hunt up."

They didn't seem eager to leave him, but did as they were told. There was something so Hugh Hefnerish to the scene, it made Anita smile. All Cavanaugh was missing was the quilted silk housecoat.

"So tell me what business you're in," he said, and reached an arm out to her.

"Let me just quickly put my costume back on." She glanced toward her small pile farther down the beach. She wanted the microphone and earpiece in place, so the others would know that she found Cavanaugh and hear the conversation.

"Better if you let the warm breeze dry you, first." He was already moving into the other direction.

She made a split second decision, linked her arm with his and went with him. There was no telling for how long the other two women would stay away and he might not want to talk business once they came back.

"My team sets up offices for companies who want a presence on the island. We do everything from finding the appropriate location to doing background checks on the staff."

"A full-service company."

"Right."

"I talked to a colleague of yours at the pageant. Samantha Hanley, I believe. And also heard about you from a friend of mine, David Granov. "

"He is a client with a broad set of requirements. We are striving to meet all of them. I hope he's satisfied." They were doing considerable money laundering for the man.

"Sings your praises," Cavanaugh said.

"And what business are you in?"

"International shipping."

"You already have an office on the island?"

"My company's headquarters are here."

"If you ever need expanding, let me know."

"I'm pondering it at the moment," he said. "Like David, I also have a broad range of needs that must be filled." He stopped and gave her a meaningful look.

His women caught up with them, dripping wet and giggling, each holding a bottle of rum and a can of caviar.

Anita kept her attention on Cavanaugh. She had him on the hook.

She repressed the excitement that bubbled up inside her and acted cool and confident. "Mind if I give you a call sometime this week to talk more about this? Maybe Monday?" she pushed.

"Call my secretary and tell her I said to squeeze you into my schedule," he said. "Will you come share in our bounty?"

She wasn't exactly sure just what that *sharing* meant. Looked like the women were pulling him toward a secluded spot on the beach. Anita was eager to tell the rest of her team about the development, that they finally had Cavanaugh. They were one step away from Tsernyakov.

They had the breakthrough they'd been hoping for, a direct-line connection to the man who had eluded all attempts of capture for the last decade. And it was their team, not professionals, who'd done it. She didn't want to waste any time before updating the others and she wanted to have her clothes on, eager for her earpiece so any further information that she could get from Cavanaugh could be heard by the rest of the team.

"I better go for my costume before the incoming tide gets it. See you later?"

"I hope so," he said, and strolled off, letting himself be steered by the women.

Anita turned to head back. She hadn't realized how far they'd walked off as they'd talked. A group of people headed toward the beach from the dance floor, shedding costumes as they walked. Except for one. The others dashed into the water and swam for the buoys. The one that still had the black costume on kept walking toward Anita. The moonlight glinted off the white skull and crossbones in the middle—the pirate flag. His movements seemed familiar. Nick? No, not tall enough.

And not a man, at all. The black vision of death was a woman, Anita realized as they got closer to each other and she could make out the shape of the body under the folds of dark cloth. The guest's face was covered with black paint.

Something in the way the woman moved made the little hairs rise at Anita's nape. She looked around for Brant. Where was he?

The guest slipped her right hand into the material, still heading straight forward. Anita slowed.

Going toward the dance floor, she would have to cross paths with the woman. She decided to listen to her instincts and not do that. Going toward the water didn't seem like the right solution, either, so she angled her feet toward the area where construction machines slept on the sand, cordoned off by yellow ribbon, waiting for the morning.

The woman changed direction, as well.

Anita walked faster, cursing herself for not being more assertive about Cavanaugh waiting for her while she dressed. As it was, she was out of the loop with no radio connection to the team.

Her pursuer picked up pace, too. She was pulling from her dress a small, black object Anita couldn't identify. She had to keep her attention on the uneven sand ahead of her, look at the jungle of machinery and figure out where she was going to go.

She glanced toward the dance floor and the beach again, but couldn't make out Brant. If Nick was one of the men, he was disguised well enough so she didn't recognize him.

She would have to save herself this time. And hadn't the mission prepared her exactly for that? She could do this, had to do this.

Get into cover. Fast.

Make a plan.

She turned back to see whether the woman

was catching up with her yet. Closer, but not yet dangerously close. Anita could clearly see now what she was holding—a gun.

Chapter Ten

Tsernyakov looked at the e-mail on his screen displaying the list of locations expected to be effected by the materials he was producing for his buyers. He had insisted on receiving the list and with good reason—it looked like The School Board's operations were about to have a serious impact on his own.

Since getting anything into the U.S. was deemed too difficult these days, The School Board had decided to release the virus at top global vacation spots for U.S. tourists and let them carry it back to their home country.

He went down the list again. Canada, Great Britain, Ireland and Australia were choice spots for those who felt uncomfortable leaving the English-speaking world. Rome and Paris were also popular destinations. Then there were the Caribbean Islands, exotic, yet still close to home.

Among these, The School Board had chosen Grand Cayman.

Tsernyakov closed the e-mail and thought about Cavanaugh. On the one hand, it would be a shame to lose him. They'd known each other for a long time and he had just taken over for Alexeev. On the other hand, they *had* known each other for a long time. The virus could present an opportunity to get rid of a man who maybe knew too much about him. Tell him to get out in time—or not? These were the kind of decisions that he was expected to make as a leader. He had a good week to think about it.

ANITA RAN between a row of machines, yellow behemoths that stood like postmodern statues silhouetted against the moonlight. Their presence made her feel comforted. Construction machinery, she knew. She'd been surrounded by them all her life. Would it be too much to hope that someone left a key in one?

She climbed an excavator. The ignition was empty. And she didn't have time to search all of them on the off chance that she succeeded. She slipped from the seat and began running again.

The music of the steel drums floated over on the evening breeze. Was it enough to cover the small sound her bare feet made on the sand?

The party had been on the other side of the property. She hadn't paid much attention to this cordoned-off area before, but she remembered that there was a rock wall somewhere to the left, separating Paradise from the next resort. At her back, toward the sea, lay open sand. Nothing to cover her on the right, either. A couple of palm trees edged two kid pools there—abandoned tonight. Beyond those spread one of the bigger pools with the swim-up bar that was full of people. Could she reach it?

Probably not. Too much open ground between here and there. Her pursuer would have a clean shot.

She needed to get behind the woman and launch her own attack, get the gun away from her somehow. She cut to the right and tried to figure out a way. A few minutes passed before she realized she couldn't circle around unseen. The gaps between the machines were too large. She would have been without cover too much of the time. And her footprints left a clear track in the sand, perfectly visible in the moonlight. She wasn't going to surprise anyone like that. She had to keep moving forward and hope for a better opportunity.

She kept low, listening for the smallest noise, glancing around every few seconds. She spotted a few smaller buildings ahead. Were they close enough to the construction machines to reach without making herself much of a target?

A bullet pinged off the front fender of the machine behind her. Anita threw herself to the sand and crawled under the vehicle. A second bullet came, missing her by an even bigger margin than the first, making just as little noise. The woman was using a silencer.

Anita crawled backward as fast as she could move. When she was all the way out on the other end, she could see the boarded-up side of what had been a small shop. A sign still proclaimed a bikini blowout sale over one window. Ten feet or so of sand separated the last machine from the store. She stopped, looked around then made a dash for it, half expecting gunshots to ring out, relieved when she made it to the other side unnoticed and unattacked.

She needed her own gun from the beach, but she had to keep in cover. A straight, flat-out run for it was out of the question. She had to get back to the rest of her team. She rounded the building and found another one close behind it—an empty, thatch-roofed bar. She vaulted over the counter and got down, searched it for anything that she could use for a weapon, but the place had been stripped empty in anticipation of the demolition.

She heard a small noise from the direction of

the shop. Whoever was after her was getting closer. She had to keep moving.

The band stopped playing and somebody was talking into the microphone, the words unintelligible from the distance. The guests cheered the announcement. Anita slipped from the bar and ran to the one-story building behind it that was attached to the hotel itself.

There was tape all over it, but she had no place else to go. To run out into the open would bring bullets. She dragged the yellow plastic ribbons aside and grabbed at the doorknob. Locked.

Diosmio.

Don't stop. Keep going. She rounded the building, breathing hard now, her heart beating wild with fear. The windows were missing from their places everywhere, but all the gaps in the wall were carefully boarded up. *The air-conditioner units.* She caught a glance of the rusty giants. She pulled herself up on the first and reached for the one above it, using the units as stepping stones to the roof. The metal made a hollow noise as she struggled. Noise that would be heard by someone nearby.

When she made it to the roof, she vaulted over the edge, picking her feet up again immediately. The tar had retained the day's heat and burned her bare soles. But what other choice did she have?

She put her feet back gingerly and swallowed the pain as she hobbled to the other side.

A sheer drop yawned below to a rock garden and the out-of-service fountain in the middle. And she couldn't come back the way she'd come. Some crazy woman with a gun was waiting for her there. Her only choice was entering the hotel itself.

The holes where the windows had been weren't blocked off here, they had probably been considered high enough to be safe from curious guests. She slipped in just as the sound of metal banging came from below. Whoever was after her was climbing the air-conditioner units.

Anita glanced around for anything she could use for a weapon, but like the bar, the room had been stripped bare. She ran out of the room into the hallway. Where was the staircase that led down?

Another loud cheer rose outside, coming from the party. Had the winner of the raffle been drawn? How long before the red button was pushed?

"Stop." The shout rang out behind her.

She froze for a split second. Then she turned.

The woman stood at the end of the hall, her feet apart, both hands on her gun.

"Who are you?"

"What did you do to William?"

She recognized the voice, at last, and stared dumbfounded at her ex-secretary. "Dee?"

"What did you do to William?" This time the words were said with slow emphasis. "What did you tell him to get him on your side? Where is he?"

"Dee, listen. This is not a good idea. They are blowing up the building."

"If William doesn't love me, do you think I care? He won't have you, either."

"William is dead," Anita bit out in desperation.

The gun wavered. "You lie." Dee dragged her mask off. She looked drawn and stressed to the limit. "The truth!" she shouted.

"He was caught. He killed himself."

Dee's face twisted in the silence that stretched between them. And, for a moment, Anita was sure she would shoot and this would be the end of it. "William is dead," she whispered.

"Because of you!" Dee shouted, and moved closer. "You broke his heart. He lost his business because of it. You made him lose everything."

"He lost his business because he gambled."

"You took the heart out of him. I put it back."

"Dee, listen to me. We have to get out of here."

"You are not going anywhere. Always high

and mighty. Always getting everything you want, getting what everyone else wants, too, and never appreciating it, never thinking twice before throwing it away."

"I'm sorry. I didn't realize you were in love with William."

"No, you didn't. Who was I to you? Nobody. Who was he to you? A toy."

"It wasn't like that." She glanced to the left, then to the right. Two more hallways. The right was a dead end.

She fixed her gaze behind Dee and nodded, not really expecting the trick to work, but Dee did turn and took the gun off her for a second. Anita used the opportunity and lunged to the side. Two bullets came in succession right behind her, but she was already in the cover of the wall.

She ran to the end of the hall, to the staircase, opened the door and nearly fell into the gaping hole below. There were no stairs.

What happened here? Then she remember her conversation with Michael. Maybe the stairs were made of steel like in her apartment building and had been removed for recycling.

She took the corridor to the right. She had to hide then get behind Dee so she could make it back to the roof of the outbuilding.

Anita opened a door to a room that was bare of

furniture like the one she'd first come through. Even the bathroom was visible at a glance. She backed out, tried another room. This one had a balcony.

She closed the door behind her and crossed the room, went outside. Could she survive a jump to the hard surface of the parking lot below? She teetered back. Too far. She crouched under the window, next to the wall, hoping that if Dee came into the room, she would just glance in from the door and move on. There was still a chance that she could get out of here.

Or maybe not.

People were chanting at the party, together, loudly. "Forty-nine. Forty-eight..."

The countdown had begun.

"So what's going on with you and Carly?" Brant asked after he'd turned his mike off.

Nick reached for his and did the same. "Nothing you need to worry about."

"Are you telling me you're not attracted to each other?" He really didn't think he'd read them wrong.

"I'm telling you I wouldn't do anything that would jeopardize the mission." Nick's voice was hard.

He obviously resented the interference. Tough.

"I suppose it wouldn't be surprising if you were attracted to her. You were the one who chose her for the mission."

"You chose Anita."

"Right," he said, and let the air out of his lungs. "Right."

Understanding dawned on Nick's face as he flashed him an amused smile.

"I'm not going to talk about it."

"I'm not asking any questions."

"It's so damn unprofessional it's making me sick."

"This mission will be over one of these days."

"You think?" He shook his head. He was getting confused about a number of things. What was happening to him?

"So," Nick said, "David Moretti picked Samantha."

Right. Sam had been the lawyer's choice, supposedly for her cat-burglary skills.

"At least David is married and nowhere near the women."

"Yeah, he has that going for him," Nick agreed.

"Who picked Gina?" Brant asked, not quite remembering.

"We picked her together. Ex-cop with plenty of training already."

He nodded. That was the way it had been.

Neither of them said anything for a while.

"I'm just saying, be careful," he told Nick.

"You, too," he responded as they turned their mikes back on.

"Gina?" He started checking in with the women.

"Nothing here," came Gina's response from the receiver.

"Sam?"

"Having fun. Nothing to report," Sam came in.

"Carly?"

"A hundred feet behind you."

"Anita?"

No response came.

"Anita?"

Nothing but silence on the line.

"Anybody seen Anita?" he asked the others.

"Not in a while," Carly said.

Where was she? "Let's walk through this party and see if we can get a visual on her. It could just be that her equipment is malfunctioning." He didn't want to alarm anyone.

"Let's go," Nick said, and started toward the dance floor.

Brant headed to the beach.

Two minutes later, he was looking at the heap her clothes made on the sand and reached down.

Where was her gun? Not in the water with her, he hoped. What would he have done? He ran his fingers through the sand and sure enough, felt something. Cloth and metal. Her earpiece was there, too. That would explain why she wasn't answering. He glanced around and when he was certain nobody was watching, he took the gun and tucked it into his waistband under his pirate coat, out of sight.

A dozen or so people were in the water around the buoys.

"Anita?" he called out over the water.

No response came.

"Anita?" he called again.

A male voice answered from the group. "Not here."

Brant looked up and down the beach, but couldn't see anyone who resembled her. "Keep looking at the party. I'll check out the edges of the property. She no longer has her costume on," he said toward his collar, giving instruction to Nick, Carly and Gina. Sam was already on the special podium. She'd won the raffle to push the button.

He walked all the way to the end of the property where a man and two blondes were having some fun in the shadow of a couple of overturned boats. He veered to the right, giving them privacy, saw the two sets of footprints on the sand that led into the jumble of construction machinery.

Anita's and someone's who was following her, or another set of lovers sneaking off in search of more fun than the party provided? He followed the tracks all the way to the other side where they disappeared on the paved area that led to a small shop and bar.

"Anita?"

Nothing but silence. A two-minute search revealed the area to be empty. In the distance the countdown had begun.

Then from the corner of his eye he caught movement behind one of the hotel's windows. He spun, but couldn't make out anything else. Had it been a trick of the lights? He didn't think so. He broke into a flat-out run toward the hotel, yelling into his microphone as he went. "Sam, do not push the button. I repeat. Do not push button. Delay."

When he reached a back entry he slammed his shoulder into the boarded-up door. It didn't even move. The two-by-fours were not impressed with his strength. The company that had secured the building had done a good job. So how had whomever he'd seen upstairs get in?

He kicked with his feet, getting more frenzied now. There came from somewhere inside him the sure knowledge that it was Anita up there and she needed him. He couldn't let anything happen to her.

He needed her, beside the mission, beyond what she was doing on the island. He needed her for himself.

He didn't have time to worry about how she was going to react to that news.

"Anita!" he shouted. "I'm here." And he ran off to find another way to get in.

ANITA PRESSED HERSELF to the wall outside on the balcony and prayed as the room's door opened. She could hear Dee take a few steps in and hesitate.

She held her breath, didn't dare move a single muscle until the door slammed behind the woman, the sound of her footsteps coming from the other side of it.

The door from the room across the hallway banged open, a moment of silence, then the door on the room to the left of Anita's, then another farther off. She waited until she could no longer hear the doors before she made her way to her room's entry.

She pushed the door open a sliver at a time until she could peek out. Dee was gone, probably trying more rooms in another hallway. Anita dashed in the opposite direction, back the way she had come, but couldn't get to where she could access the roof. Dee was in that hallway now. So Anita opened the door to the staircase. If she could somehow lower herself, there might be a way to get outside from the lower level.

She needed a rope.

She glanced around, desperate for one, but couldn't see anything that could have been any kind of substitute. Then she spotted some coated wires hanging from the wall and dashed over to them, grabbing a hold of the end and pulling with all she was worth. After a few seconds, she realized it wasn't going to work. Even if the cable held her weight, the plastic coating was too slippery to hang on to.

The doors on the other side were now banging just around the corner. Dee was coming back.

Anita jumped into the nearest room. It didn't have a balcony. And it was too late to get out now and try to find another place to hide. She stepped into the shower behind the bathroom door.

A few seconds passed before Dee came in, this time walking farther into the room. Anita took advantage of it and came up behind her, hurling herself on the woman.

"You don't have to do this, Dee. We can just walk away," she said as they rolled on the floor.

Dee only grunted in response, her face red with effort as she struggled to keep control of the gun.

"William would want you to live," Anita said in final desperation, grasping for anything that might stop her.

But rather than calming down, an even more fierce rage contorted Dee's face. "Don't you dare talk to me about William."

Anita heard her name called from somewhere outside. Brant's voice.

The second of surprise and relief cost her. Dee managed to get on top, with her full weight on Anita, squishing her chest so she couldn't get a response out.

They struggled for several long seconds and Dee somehow managed to get the gun between them. She squeezed the trigger twice.

Anita waited for the pain but it didn't come, so she flipped the woman over. Was Dee hurt? From the way she was still fighting it didn't seem likely.

Both bullets had missed.

She put her index finger over Dee's on the trigger and forced the gun higher. Dee struggled hard enough to set off another shot that drilled into the ceiling above them, showering them with drywall dust. Then the weapon was finally in Anita's hands.

She backed away from Dee and took a step toward the door. The woman came right after her.

"Stop. I'll shoot. I'm not kidding."

Dee lunged for her as if she hadn't even heard her. The click echoed in the room. The magazine was empty.

From the look of Dee's face, she hadn't been counting the bullets, either.

She dropped the gun and hooked her right fist under Dee's jaw just as she had learned from Nick during her initial training at Quantico.

Diosmio, that hurt.

Dee staggered back, surprise on her face.

Anita didn't wait for her to regain her balance. She ran from the room. The building was about to come down any second. She had to get out.

"Brant!" She called his name at the top of her lungs. Was he still here, or had he left?

She heard the sound of a motor outside and she ran to the next room to look out. Brant was aiming for the hotel on the back of a four-wheeler. Was he trying to get in through a lower entrance?

"Brant!" She called his name again, but he couldn't hear her over the noise of the motor. "No!" She no longer cared if she gave away her location to Dee.

The staircases were gone. Even if Brant got in down there, he couldn't get up here. And if he got stuck looking for her, the only result would be that he would blow up with the building, too.

She had to get his attention.

Anita scoured the room. Nothing but a few pieces of busted drywall littered the floor. She ran with one to the balcony and tossed it, missed completely. But the second piece fell directly in front of Brant and drew his attention up.

He drove the four-wheeler to under her balcony.

"Jump!"

He was standing free now, holding his arms out.

Diosmio, the distance was a long one between them. What if he didn't catch her? Construction rubble littered the paved area around the hotel. If she fell on that—

The door banged open behind her. Dee was holding a shower rod in her hand, looking absolutely raving mad and capable of anything.

Anita didn't have time to climb the brick railing. She pitched forward head first and threw her weight over. Then she crashed through the air, trusting that Brant would be there at the end.

She came down hard, taking him with her. He never even paused, but got up and helped her onto the back of the four-wheeler and spun the machine around, racing toward the cement barricades the demolition company had erected on the street front to protect the road. If they could get behind that— They were barely a couple dozen feet away when the place went down, the noise of the explosion deafening her, the force of it knocking her to the ground.

Brant rolled with her, made sure he was on top of her as the four-wheeler raced away on its own now, bombarded with debris like they were.

A minute or two passed before she could lift up her head and look toward the heap that had very nearly taken both of them out.

"Dee." She couldn't hear the word she whispered from the ringing in her ears.

Brant rolled off her with a groan that rumbled through his chest rather than came out of his mouth. Anita tried to stand, but he put a restraining hand on her arm.

"Are you hurt?"

She followed his gaze to her bloody leg. She wiped away the dust-caked blood and revealed a six-inch gash on the outside of her left thigh.

Brant picked her up, none too steady on his own feet, his lips set in a tight line. His face was closed, unreadable. She could only guess his emotion by the strength with which he held her to his chest as he walked with her toward the barricades.

"I might want to breathe," she said. "Like once a minute or so."

His mood didn't seem to lighten, although he did loosen his hold on her.

"Really, I'm okay."

He gave a slight shake of the head. "I'm too old for this."

He didn't look too old for anything just then, covered in dust and carrying her through the rubble, having saved her just moments ago. To her, he looked very much like a hero.

Chapter Eleven

Brant was leaving. He hadn't even come into the office today.

Anita stared at the numbers on the screen as she grappled with the thought.

Her laptop beeped with an instant message. From Brant.

"Are you in the office?"

"All morning." She typed the response. "My first outside meeting is after lunch."

"I'll pop over. Got good news."

She wanted to ask what good news, but he had signed off already.

He was coming over. She resisted the urge to run to the bathroom to refresh her makeup. He was leaving the island soon—a depressing and disheartening thought.

He had good news.

Good news would be if he had suddenly realized that he was in love with her and couldn't live without her. The scene that flashed through her mind was a lot like those South-American soap operas she loved to hate.

Not likely, she thought. He wasn't the fanciful type. He was reasonable and thought things out, steady, solid—qualities that drew her to him. He was an honorable man. And he was sexy. She tried not to dwell on just how sexy, how incredible those kisses were that they had shared. No point in torturing herself. Another lip-lock wasn't likely to happen between them again.

He was leaving.

She hated how much the thought hurt.

She wanted more of him, to get to know him better, spend more time together on the beach, in his car, in his hotel room…

She pushed her chair away from her desk, wishing she could push her thoughts away just as easily. She got up to go to the kitchen for a bottle of water from the fridge. She needed a few minutes to get her thoughts together before he got here. Otherwise, he would take one look at her and figure out something was up. No way was she going to explain what was wrong with her now.

But she didn't have much time to gather herself. He was coming through the door by the time she was done fidgeting in the kitchen. His hotel was just across the road from the office.

"Hi. How is the leg?" His mahogany eyes looked her over.

She felt naked in the modest, silk skirtsuit. "Fine. It pulls a little. I'm sure it would pull more if they'd used stitches instead of the emergency glue thing."

"Best invention since the Magnum Grill," he said, sounding like someone who spoke from experience.

Gina and Carly were coming from their offices.

"Good work last night," he told them both.

"You, too," Gina said. "Nice rescue."

Sam sailed through the door with a box of printer paper. "We're back in business. Hi."

He took the box from her and carried it to its spot.

"Thanks for holding off with the button," he said.

"No problem. Anita already offered me a lifetime supply of homemade salsa."

He glanced back at Anita with a thin smile. "Sign me onto that list."

And her foolish heart thumped at his words. Did that mean they might have contact beyond the mission?

"Paramedics give you a hard time?" Brant turned back to Sam.

She shook her head. "Just told me to stay out of the sun for a few days. I'm a good fainter." She grinned.

Her sudden pretend weakness had worked great for delaying the demolition. To a point. Unfortunately, as they were pushing back people to let her have some air, one of the paramedics managed to step on the button in the confusion—a scene they had discussed in great detail that morning.

If the button had been pushed just a minute or two earlier— It was a pretty uncomfortable feeling to know that she owed her life to a coincidence.

No, not coincidence. She corrected herself. She owed her life to Brant. He had risked his own to come after her and save her.

"So do you want to hear your good news in private or here and now?" Brant was asking her.

She felt a rush of disappointment. If "public" was an option, she supposed the news wasn't, *I love you and I want to make you mine.*

"Here and now is good," she said.

"I just heard from David Moretti." David was the lawyer who represented the women in the deal they had made with the authorities. "Your conviction has been officially thrown out by a federal appeals court." He smiled.

And then she was smiling, too, feeling as if a crushing weight had lifted off her shoulders. Her name was cleared. She had wanted this more than she had ever wanted anything in her life. "Thank you."

"I haven't done much," he said. "Congratulations."

"Congratulations." Carly came over for a hug.

Gina grinned as she patted Anita on the shoulder. "That quick?" she asked Brant.

He flashed a mysterious smile.

"Must be nice to have friends in high places." Gina smiled back.

"Way to go," Sam was saying.

"Moretti will come down in a couple of days. He has papers for you to sign," Brant went on. "Looks like you might also get some kind of compensation from the government for the wrongful conviction, provided that you are willing to sign a release that says you won't sue them."

"Does she get to keep the four mil in addition to the compensation?" Carly asked, struggling with a grin. "We're best friends, right?"

"Very funny," Anita said, but she *could* actually smile about it now.

"How about going out to celebrate tonight?" Gina suggested. "Brant, coming with us?"

Anita stilled as she waited for his answer. He

shook his head, but she thought she saw regret in his eyes.

"I'm flying back to the States this evening. I'm already packed."

The words fell on her like the sharp debris from the exploding hotel, hurting more than she had expected.

"Have a good trip," she said, but couldn't pull off the smile she was trying to force.

He was watching her. "Thank you. There is one more thing."

She wasn't sure if she wanted to hear more. She wanted to go into her office and close the door and allow herself to be just miserable for ten minutes.

"Since your situation has changed considerably from the time you had agreed to the mission— What I am saying is that, we cannot hold you to the agreement. If you want to leave—"

"I don't."

His shoulders relaxed. "Okay. Thank you."

"Just can't stand us having all the fun, can you?" Carly teased, but she looked relieved, too. All the women did.

"Once people get to know us—" Gina said matter-of-factly as she looked around at the team "—they often find they can't live without us. It's all the charisma and magnetism."

Brant grinned. "I'm going to miss you, ladies, and that's a fact."

Anita took a slow breath. She didn't want to think about just how much she was going to miss him.

WHEN WAS his flight leaving? Anita beeped the horn, trying to get through the jumble of traffic that was backed up for blocks due to the jazz festival starting on the beach.

What was she doing trying to get to Brant?

She wasn't sure, only knew that she had to see him one more time; that watching him walk out of the office couldn't be the last contact they had.

He had said she needed to learn to fight for herself. That was exactly what she was doing. She was going to fight for herself and for him.

The bottleneck finally cleared up ahead and she made it through the intersection. She didn't bother looking for a parking space, just pulled over in front of the hotel, shut off the car and ran for the bank of elevators in the back of the lobby.

Was it just her or was the elevator slower than ever before?

Hours seemed to pass before she stepped out on his floor. She knocked on the door of his room. "Brant?"

She held her breath, something squeezing tight in her chest when no response came.

She banged again and ignored the maid who watched her from the end of the hallway. "Brant?"

Please be here.

She waited awhile then turned toward the maid. "Do you know if the man who had this room checked out?"

"Sorry, ma'am. That room is not on my list. I only clean up to 910. But checkout is by noon. Late checkout is by two."

Anita glanced at her watch, although she had a fair idea of the time. She'd gotten all the way home from work before she realized she couldn't let him go without trying to talk to him. Then wasted precious time trying to talk herself out of it first. And then there was the endless traffic. It was now after seven.

She was too late. He had left.

She blinked away the tears of frustration and pain from her eyes, leaned her head against the door for a second. She'd missed him. Why hadn't she come earlier?

When the door opened, she nearly fell in.

Brant looked at her with concern; he was naked save a white towel around his hips.

She tumbled in, into his arms, against his wide chest, unable to think of a single word she was going to say.

"Are you okay?" He put his arms around her and let the door shut behind them.

"I thought you were gone."

"I was in the shower," he said, and pulled back so he could look at her. "I decided to stay an extra night. I wanted to have another chance to talk with you."

The relief that was still flooding her added to the feel of him practically naked holding her in his arms, took her breath away.

"Are you okay?" he asked again.

She pressed her lips to his.

He took them gently, but didn't deepen the kiss and pulled away after a short while. "I think we should talk before—"

Great. The one man who wanted to talk before and she had to pick him.

"You told me truth always triumphs in the end," she said. "The truth is, I think I'm falling in love with you. I don't want to never see you again."

"That's what I was going to talk to you about. Give me a second to get dressed."

She closed her eyes for a second, then drew away and nodded. If he wanted to get dressed, what he wanted to tell her wasn't what she wanted to tell him. Because one of the things she would have really liked from the man she was falling in love with was for him to be naked, now, with her on the bed.

She had misread him. How was that possible? How big of a fool was she? Had she been away from society and normal relationships for so long that her judgment had failed her completely?

She swallowed the disappointment and the pain. "I better get down there and get my car out of illegal parking. I'll wait for you in the lobby." She couldn't look at him as she walked out.

He was down in ten minutes, dressed in shorts and an island shirt, looking better than a man who was about to give her the brush-off should.

"Ready?"

She nodded.

He led her through to the parking garage, jiggling his keys. Was he nervous?

"Where are we going?"

"Can't tell you. But man, I hope you'll like it."

His lips stretched into a nervous smile. The first nervous smile she'd seen on Brant Law. She wouldn't have thought anything could get him rattled.

She became only more puzzled when he turned toward the ocean after pulling out from parking. "All the major roads that go to Seven Mile Beach are plugged with traffic."

"We're going to the marina," he said.

He wanted to go boating now? Then she remembered his passion for everything that ran on
water. "You bought a boat?"

"You'll have to wait and see," he said.

He had splurged on some water-wonder and he
was bringing her out to show it to her because he
considered her a friend. She should have been
happy. At least he considered her as something.
She swallowed the urge to bang her head into
the dashboard and decided not to ask any further
questions. She wasn't sure how long she could
contain her disappointment. It would have been
nice to hang on to some dignity, at least.

They were at the marina in fifteen minutes. He
had a WaveRunner rented in another five.

"You wanted to show me the ocean?" she
asked, but got on behind him.

"Give me a few more minutes," he said as he
headed straight out.

Maybe he'd gone loopy, hit his head when they
went down with the hotel. Did concussions have
weird symptoms like this? Delayed reaction?

"Want to switch? I wouldn't mind driving."

"You don't know where we're going."

She wondered if he did.

But then he cut the motor and turned around,
turned her toward the beach instead of the ocean.
The sun was just going down over the row of

villas in the back of the private beaches. The sight was breathtaking.

"Okay, first things first. I arranged for a secure phone for you for tomorrow morning. You can call your family if you want. Just don't mention the mission. You will still have to keep your cover."

Tears clouded her eyes; she couldn't believe that he had set this up. Lord, it had been a long time since she had called home. "Thank you." She swallowed hard, but couldn't keep smiling.

He turned her gently and pointed to the shore. "Now about item number two on tonight's to-do list. You are not going to ask me what we are looking at?"

She was definitely driving back. "The sunset?"

He shook his head and pointed again. And she recognized the hangout from the other night where they had parked on the beach while they'd watched Cavanaugh's boat come in.

"My new house," he said.

And she was wondering if she, too, was getting loopy, or if she misunderstood him. "What do you mean?"

"I rented it. I'm going to stick close by for a while longer. Not that I don't trust the team or Nick to get the job done. It's just that—" he hesitated "—this mission is too important, perhaps the most important thing I've done in my career. And you are… You are quickly becoming the most important woman in my life."

This time he didn't wait for her to throw herself into his arms, but moved in and kissed her with the same hope and passion that had been in his voice.

And all she could feel was poignant pleasure; all she could think was that Brant had rearranged his life so he could be close to her.

Nothing had ever been as good as his lips on hers. She snuggled closer and buried herself in his warmth and his strength and his desire for her that she was now close enough to feel.

"I want you," he mumbled the admission against her lips.

"It's good to be on the same page," she said.

"We should probably wait until the mission is over and our relationship is not so complicated."

"It's not complicated now. I'm no longer a convict on probation. I'm a volunteer," she said, and slid her hands under his shirt.

"What are you doing to me?"

She would have thought that was obvious, but spelled it out just to be clear. "Fighting for what I want."

"Then by all means, keep up the good fight." He pulled her onto his lap.

For a long heated moment or two she was thinking she could stay like that forever. But it wasn't true, her need for him was growing, pushing her for more, bringing an urgency she had trouble controlling.

And why should she? She lifted her arms when he tugged at the bottom of her halter top, helped him pull it over her head.

"You don't have a bra on," he said on a choked voice.

"The top had one of those elastic things built in."

"Best invention since—ever." He leaned back to allow her to help him out of his shirt.

He lifted his hands to her arms to caress them, his strong, warm fingers gliding across her skin. When he finally cupped her breasts, she leaned back to offer him better access. She wanted more of him, all of him, forever.

The WaveRunner wobbled under them, rocked by the water. She felt perfectly safe with him. She always had, she realized, since she had first met Brant.

His hands slid down to encircle her waist and slowly slipped off the short wraparound skirt she wore, then stopped as he had just caught himself, realized what he was doing. "Should we go out to shore?"

Did she want to wait a minute longer? Definitely not.

She drew her legs up between them and divested herself of her underwear.

"Good choice," he said as he performed a pretty interesting bit of acrobatics to get rid of his shorts.

Then he pulled her back onto his lap again, facing each other, nestled against each other's bodies, making a perfect unit as they melted together. He dipped his mouth to her breast and savored one nipple then the other.

Oh, that—that— She squirmed against him as heat flooded her in a couple of strategic places.

He had a magnificent body. She began exploring it shyly at first, then became more and more brazen. Her fingers glided across smooth cords of muscle as they shifted under his skin with every move he made. She loved the breadth of his shoulders, the smattering of fine hairs across his chest—everything about the way he felt under her hands.

She wanted to spend hours discovering him like this, having him discover her in turn. Hours, weeks, years.

But at the same time a tidal wave of urgency was rushing to shore inside her body. She wanted him, now, now, now. She shifted closer on instinct, blindly seeking the release his mouth on her breast was promising.

He seemed to receive her silent message because he slid his hands under her bottom and lifted her up, over and onto him.

She arched her head back as pleasure sliced into her sharp and overpowering before slowly disbursing to every cell.

Then he moved.

For the first few thrusts, she could do nothing but hang on to his shoulders for support. Then the urgency returned and she began to move with him with the perfect unity of the planets moving together.

"I'm glad I didn't know it could be like this," he said on a rasp voice. "You've driven me half-crazy as it is."

"I might have entertained a few fantasies about you," she admitted.

"Like what?"

She made him wait for it.

"There was a bodyguard-to-the-rescue scenario."

He groaned.

She was smiling as she went on. "Then the whole James Bondish love in an escape pod in the middle of a spy mission thing."

He pressed deep inside her. "A healthy imagination is a thing to be encouraged."

"You didn't expect this much creativity from an accountant, did you?" she teased.

"I've come to expect just about anything from you," he said.

Then he picked up pace and both of them fell silent, in a mad race toward something unnamable all of a sudden, toward the sunset or the world beyond it, toward forever and happiness and a sheer physical joy that left them breathless.

It didn't seem like the pleasure that raked her body could get more intense and more immediate, but he managed it somehow with every thrust.

"Brant." His name tore from her lips.

His gaze melted into hers. "I know." His voice was so rough it came out barely above a whisper.

Then she lost track of time for a while.

When they came apart, into tiny pieces so they seemed one and the same, particles of light floating, glinting on top of an ocean of pleasure, she cried his name again, with desperate passion this time and he kissed her, kept kissing her until they were slumped against each other, weak and giddy and only half-believing the intensity of what had just happened.

I've missed this, she thought, just as he said, "I've missed you."

She was correcting herself that she couldn't have possibly missed *this,* because she had never experienced anything remotely like this before, when the meaning of his words finally reached her pleasure-fogged brain.

"How could you miss me? You didn't know me before," she asked against the warm skin of his neck then looked up into his turbulent eyes.

"I meant—" He looked away with the most endearing embarrassed expression.

"What?"

"There's nothing worse than a sappy FBI agent," he said gruffly.

"I love sappy FBI agents." She smiled.

He held her tighter. "Better make it just *this* one."

"I love *this* sappy FBI agent."

Everything seemed to stop around them, the waves, the breeze, the seagulls in the air.

"Sometimes it seems like I've been waiting for you forever," he said, then winced. "I better balance that with something macho."

"Right." She grinned, her knees still deliciously weak, her body sated to the point of feeling like quivering Jell-O. "You have a reputation to uphold."

He looked into her eyes deep and long. "I love you more than I love the combustion engine."

"You sure know how to turn a woman's head,"

she said over the mad thumping her heart insisted on all of a sudden.

"I want us to be like this forever," he said, then gave a twisted smile. "Oh, man. Was that sappy again?"

Her heart did a big slow roll in her chest. She lifted her lips to his. "Nothing wrong with sappy. I love sappy." She wouldn't have minded a whole lifetime of it.

And his eyes promised that and more.

"I love you," he said just before he kissed her.

* * * * *

Look for more MISSION: REDEMPTION
*titles from Dana Marton later in 2007,
only in Harlequin Intrigue!*

Mediterranean Nights

Join the guests and crew of Alexandra's Dream,
*the newest luxury ship to set sail on the
romantic Mediterranean, as they experience
the glamorous world of cruising.*

*A new Harlequin continuity series
begins in June 2007 with
FROM RUSSIA, WITH LOVE
by Ingrid Weaver.*

*Marina Artamova books a cabin on the
luxurious cruise ship* Alexandra's Dream,
*when she finds out that her orphaned nephew
and his adoptive father are aboard. She's
determined to be reunited with the boy...but
the romantic ambience of the ship and
her undeniable attraction to a man she
considers her enemy are about to
interfere with her quest!*

Turn the page for a sneak preview!

Piraeus, Greece

"THERE SHE IS, Stefan. *Alexandra's Dream.*" David Anderson squatted beside his new son and pointed at the dark blue hull that towered above the pier. The cruise ship was a majestic sight, twelve decks high and as long as a city block. A circle of silver and gold stars, the logo of the Liberty cruise line, gleamed from the swept-back smokestack. Like some legendary sea creature born for the water, the ship emanated power from every sleek curve— even at rest it held the promise of motion. "That's going to be our home for the next ten days."

The child beside him remained silent, his cheeks working in and out as he sucked furiously on his thumb. Hair so blond it appeared white ruffled against his forehead in the harbor breeze. The baby-sweet scent unique to the very young mingled with the tang of the sea.

"Ship," David said. "Uh, *parakhod*."

From beneath his bangs, Stefan looked at the *Alexandra's Dream*. Although he didn't release his thumb, the corners of his mouth tightened with the beginning of a smile.

David grinned. That was Stefan's first smile this afternoon, one of only two since they had left the orphanage yesterday. It was probably because of the boat—according to the orphanage staff, the boy loved boats, which was the main reason David had decided to book this cruise. Then again, there was a strong possibility the smile could have been a reaction to David's attempt at pocket-dictionary Russian. Whatever the cause, it was a good start.

The liaison from the adoption agency had claimed that Stefan had been taught some English, but David had yet to see evidence of it. David continued to speak, positive his son would understand his tone even if he couldn't grasp the words. "This is her maiden voyage. Her first trip, just like this is our first trip, and that makes it special." He motioned toward the stage that had been set up on the pier beneath the ship's bow. "That's why everyone's celebrating."

The ship's official christening ceremony had been held the day before and had been a closed affair, with only the cruise-line executives and

VIP guests invited, but the stage hadn't yet been disassembled. Banners bearing the blue and white of the Greek flag of the ship's owner, as well as the Liberty circle of stars logo, draped the edges of the platform. In the center, a group of musicians and a dance troupe dressed in traditional white folk costumes performed for the benefit of the *Alexandra's Dream*'s first passengers. Their audience was in a festive mood, snapping their fingers in time to the music while the dancers twirled and wove through their steps.

David bobbed his head to the rhythm of the mandolins. They were playing a folk tune that seemed vaguely familiar, possibly from a movie he'd seen. He hummed a few notes. "Catchy melody, isn't it?"

Stefan turned his gaze on David. His eyes were a striking shade of blue, as cool and pale as a winter horizon and far too solemn for a child not yet five. Still, the smile that hovered at the corners of his mouth persisted. He moved his head with the music, mirroring David's motion.

David gave a silent cheer at the interaction. Hopefully, this cruise would provide countless opportunities for more. "Hey, good for you," he said. "Do you like the music?"

The child's eyes sparked. He withdrew his thumb with a pop. *"Moozika!"*

"Music. Right!" David held out his hand. "Come on, let's go closer so we can watch the dancers."

Stefan grasped David's hand quickly, as if he feared it would be withdrawn. In an instant his budding smile was replaced by a look close to panic.

Did he remember the car accident that had killed his parents? It would be a mercy if he didn't. As far as David knew, Stefan had never spoken of it to anyone. Whatever he had seen had made him run so far from the crash that the police hadn't found him until the next day. The event had traumatized him to the extent that he hadn't uttered a word until his fifth week at the orphanage. Even now he seldom talked.

David sat back on his heels and brushed the hair from Stefan's forehead. That solemn, too-old gaze locked with his and, for an instant, David felt as if he looked back in time at an image of himself thirty years ago.

He didn't need to speak the same language to understand exactly how this boy felt. He knew what it meant to be alone and powerless among strangers, trying to be brave and tough but wishing with every fiber of his being for a place to belong, to be safe and, most of all, for someone to love him....

He knew in his heart he would be a good parent to Stefan. It was why he had never considered halting the adoption process after Ellie had left him. He hadn't balked when he'd learned of the recent claim by Stefan's spinster aunt, either; the absentee relative had shown up too late for her case to be considered. The adoption was meant to be. He and this child already shared a bond that went deeper than paperwork or legalities.

A seagull screeched overhead, making Stefan start and press closer to David.

"That's my boy," David murmured. He swallowed hard, struck by the simple truth of what he had just said.

That's my *boy.*

"I CAN'T BE PATIENT, RUDOLPH. I'm not going to stand by and watch my nephew get ripped from his country and his roots to live on the other side of the world."

Rudolph hissed out a slow breath. "Marina, I don't like the sound of that. What are you planning?"

"I'm going to talk some sense into this American kidnapper."

"No. Absolutely not. No offence, but diplomacy is not your strong suit."

"Diplomacy be damned. Their ship's due to sail at five o'clock."

"Then you wouldn't have an opportunity to speak with him even if his lawyer agreed to a meeting."

"I'll have ten days of opportunities, Rudolph, since I plan to be on board that ship."

* * * * *

*Follow Marina and David as they join forces
to uncover the reason behind little Stefan's
unusual silence and the secret behind
the death of his parents....*

*Look for FROM RUSSIA, WITH LOVE
by Ingrid Weaver
in stores June 2007.*

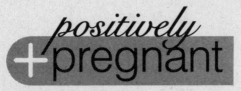

SPECIAL EDITION™

COMING IN JUNE

HER LAST FIRST DATE

by *USA TODAY* bestsellling author

SUSAN MALLERY

After one too many bad dates, Crissy Phillips
finally swore off men. Recently widowed,
pediatrician Josh Daniels can't risk losing his
heart. With an intense attraction pulling them
together, will their fear keep them apart?
Or will one wild night change everything...?

positively +pregnant

Sometimes the unexpected
is the best news of all....

REQUEST YOUR FREE BOOKS!

2 FREE NOVELS PLUS 2 FREE GIFTS!

HARLEQUIN®

INTRIGUE®

Breathtaking Romantic Suspense

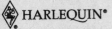
HARLEQUIN®

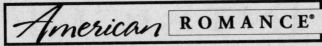
American ROMANCE®

is proud to present a special treat this
Fourth of July with three stories
to kick off your summer!

SUMMER LOVIN'
by
Marin Thomas,
Laura Marie Altom
Ann Roth

This year, celebrating the Fourth of July in Silver Cliff,
Colorado, is going to be special. There's an all-year
high school reunion taking place before the old
school building gets torn down. As old flames find
each other and new romances begin, this small
town is looking like the perfect place
for some summer lovin'!

Available June 2007
wherever Harlequin books are sold.

www.eHarlequin.com   HAR75169

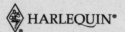

HARLEQUIN®

INTRIGUE®

COMING NEXT MONTH

#993 HIGH SOCIETY SABOTAGE by Kathleen Long
Bodyguards Unlimited, Denver, CO (Book 4 of 6)
In order to blend into the world of CEO Stephen Turner, PPS agent Sara Montgomery adopts the role she left behind years ago—debutante—to stop investors from dying.

#994 ROYAL LOCKDOWN by Rebecca York
Lights Out (Book 1 of 4)
A brand-new continuity! Princess Ariana LeBron brought the famous Beau Pays sapphire to Boston, which security expert Shane Peters intended to steal. But plans changed when an act of revenge plunged Boston into a complete blackout.

#995 COLBY VS. COLBY by Debra Webb
Colby Agency: The Equalizers (Book 3 of 3)
Does the beginning of the Equalizers mean the end of the Colby Agency? Jim Colby and Victoria Camp-Colby go head-to-head when they both send agents to L.A., where nothing is as simple as it seems.

#996 SECRET OF DEADMAN'S COULEE by B.J. Daniels
Whitehorse, Montana
A downed plane in Missouri Breaks badlands was bad enough. But on board was someone who was murdered thirty-two years ago? Sheriff Carter Jackson and Eve Bailey thought their reunion would be hard enough....

#997 SHOWDOWN WITH THE SHERIFF by Jan Hambright
Sheriff Logan Brewer called Rory Matson back to Reaper's Point, not to identify her father's body, but the skull discovered in his backpack at the time of his death.

#998 FORBIDDEN TEMPTATION by Paula Graves
Women were dying in Birmingham's trendy nightclub district, and only Rose Browning saw a killer's pattern emerging. But she didn't know how to stop him, not until hot-shot criminal profiler Daniel Hartman arrived.

www.eHarlequin.com

HICNM0507